A CORPSE IN THE CAFE

A FRENCH QUARTER MYSTERY

JEN PITTS

For Dave
Thanks for being my partner in crime

CONTENTS

1

I love coffee anytime. Inhaling the irresistible aroma of coffee, listening to the invigorating sounds of grinding espresso beans and then the thunderous whoosh of the espresso being brewed, and the first drops of the coffee into the mug bring me joy. Add the intoxicating scent of warm sweet potato scones, and I'm in heaven.

Libby Tyler asked me to help at tonight's art show opening. I didn't hesitate to say yes. Not just for the coffee and my favorite pastries, but she is a friend. And yes, she's my landlord and my boyfriend's mother. But Libby was also the unofficial mother to everyone who lived at Thibodeaux Mansion, and when Momma asks for help, everyone says yes.

People knew Libby's café, Artistic Coffee and Creations, as the best neighborhood café for coffee, pastries, and art. She rarely showcased her own work, instead focusing on promoting others in the community. Libby normally didn't offer shows to out-of-town artists, but Tessa Ferguson asked Libby to make an exception for her former professor, Griffin Blackthorn. Tessa, a budding photographer, took art classes with him at Southern Pines University before she moved to New Orleans.

"Good help is hard to find, especially a barista that can bake, so I said yes. Tessa insisted Griffin is moving to New Orleans after he finishes teaching this semester," Libby had explained.

Libby tasked me with refilling the creamer-and-sugar sets, along with the noncaloric sugar packet caddy on each table. Although Libby preferred real sugar, she had to cater to the demand for the fake stuff in the yellow packets. But first I decided to help her with the "talent," which is how I ended up joining her and Griffin. Although Libby was in mid-sentence, Griffin had turned his attention to me when I joined them.

"Darling, who might you be?" Griffin offered his hand. "I'm Griffin. Which of my paintings do you like best?"

"I'm Samantha Richardson, and I haven't picked a favorite yet." As a painter I expected him to have paint-stained and rough hands, but he could have been a hand model by the softness of his skin and his immaculate manicure.

"Let me give you a personal tour of my work. *Moonshine Melancholy* is one of my favorites, but I would enjoy painting you. Your beautiful red hair and glimmering eyes are captivating. *Southern Seductress* is the perfect title." Griffin tilted his head from side to side as if he were studying my face. "Why don't you just give me your number? I'll call you to schedule a time for you to come and sit for me."

Before I could decline his offer to pose for him, if that was what he was actually offering, Libby stepped in between us. The silver streak in her auburn hair had come loose from her ponytail, and the positive energy that normally exuded from her petite frame had disappeared.

"Let's get back to our discussion, Griffin. Not every party in New Orleans is about cocktails and throwing beads," Libby explained through gritted teeth. Griffin entered the café with expectations as grand and theatrical as his artwork on the walls.

"I assumed an evening art show would serve alcohol, especially with so many of my paintings referencing moonshine." Griffin shrugged his shoulders, but his nonchalant attitude didn't carry through to his intense gaze around the café. His hair grazed the shoulders of his tight, black T-shirt that was tucked into a pair of black jeans. The streaks of gray in his hair and goatee, along with the slight crow's-feet around his eyes, made me believe he was in his late forties.

"As I explained on our video chat, we're a café, and we don't serve cocktails. It's never been a problem for any of the other hundreds of art shows I've hosted. I'm sure Tessa explained that to you, too." Libby sighed and smoothed down her apron, which I recognized as her way of keeping herself from saying, "Bless your heart." Before I moved to New Orleans nine months ago, I assumed that was a term of endearment. Occasionally it's used that way, but most times it's letting someone know they're none too bright.

Instead of blessing Griffin's heart, Libby said, "I don't offer alcohol here, just coffee, juice, tea, and good old-fashioned water. We're not open at night usually, and I don't have a liquor license."

"You weren't joking, then? I've always found a cocktail or three loosens checkbooks." Griffin laughed. "No, I can see you aren't, Libby. I'm sure it will be a lovely evening, anyway."

"I'm so glad you approve." Libby smiled, but the tension in her neck was obvious.

A smile crossed Griffin's face, so he apparently hadn't

caught Libby's sarcasm. Or if he had, he was ignoring it. "I'll just check on all the information plaques by the paintings to make sure they're correct. Especially the prices."

Griffin sauntered off to the far end of the café and stood in front of his favorite painting, *Moonshine Melancholy*. The moon peeked out from behind a tall row of trees that framed a clearing in the forest. Three mason jars sat on a log in a clearing in a dense forest. Two more jars lay toppled over, a clear liquid oozed out onto the mossy ground. Losing the moonshine must have been the melancholy in the title, since the rich colors of the painting added a liveliness to the dark scene.

Some guests had already arrived at the café, even though the party was still twenty minutes away. Most of the guests were either friends, neighbors, or fellow business owners whom I knew or recognized from previous art shows, but Suzy Landry's arrival surprised me. Dressed in a soft-yellow sweater and turquoise pencil skirt, she took off the matching scarf covering her head. She shook out her silky black hair, so the curls settled across her shoulders. She owned Suzy's Surprises, a gift store located across the street from my shop, Lagniappe Books. Suzy had never come to one of Libby's shows before tonight.

I didn't have a chance to talk to her or anyone else as I hurried to finish putting out the sugar-and-creamer sets. As I worked, I looked for Griffin, expecting him to be greeting the guests. As I finished, Griffin came out from the restroom.

Libby beelined to Griffin and pointed to the bakery counter. Tessa had just come out of the kitchen. She carried a tray of sweet potato scones from the kitchen to the prep area behind the bakery counter. Libby waved her over.

"Tessa, darling, Griffin is here!" Libby shouted.

"Griffin! I'm so glad you made it!" Tessa rushed out from

behind the bakery counter. Her high-heel boots clicked on the black-and-white tile floor until she reached Griffin. She opened her arms out as if she was going to hug him, but Griffin took a step backward.

"Tessa, darling, your apron has flour all over it. I'll look like I was eating beignets at Café du Monde if I get white powder all over my outfit." Griffin laughed and leaned his head toward Tessa. I braced myself for him to give her a passionate kiss, based on the leer he gave her. Instead, he kissed her chastely on the cheek.

Tessa blushed and smiled. She didn't look disappointed by his lack of romantic affection, which I assumed she would be, based on the excitement she displayed running over to him.

"Sorry, I forget I'm wearing this apron all the time." Tessa wiped her hands on the apron and then brushed the wisps of pink hair out of her eyes. Her already five feet, ten inches made her even more statuesque, especially with the rest of her pastel hair pulled back in a topknot on her head.

"Hopefully, you're not wearing it when you're out on photography assignments," Griffin said.

"Wait until you see the incredible photos Tessa took of your paintings here in the café." Libby put her arm around Tessa's waist. "She's such a talented photographer."

"Thanks, Libby." Tessa blushed again and pulled on the hem of her formfitting purple dress.

"She was my best student," Griffin said.

"Tessa surely was *one* of your best students." Suzy had snuck up behind us.

"Suzy, darling, you're here!" Griffin wrapped his arms around her waist and kissed her on the lips.

"Of course I am," Suzy said as they parted. "I'm your wife. I wouldn't miss this for the world."

2

———————

Libby and I looked at each other and mouthed, "Did you know?" and then both shook our heads.

I talked to Suzy almost every day when I worked at my shop, Lagniappe Books. We've talked about the economy, the weather, the latest parade to go down Royal Street, and who has the best muffuletta sandwiches—everything except for the fact she had a husband.

"Griffin, didn't you mention we were married when you set this show up?" Suzy turned to a pale-faced Tessa. "You didn't tell them, either, Tessa? You realize we are still married, don't you?"

Suzy's question, or rather, statement, appeared to be directed at Griffin more than Tessa. But Tessa answered Suzy. She grasped the sides of her apron and said, "Yes, I do. I need to get back to work. It's going to be a successful show, Griffin."

Tessa turned on her heels and charged toward the bakery counter.

"Griffin, you never told me you were married to Suzy." Libby looked at him, dumbfounded.

"Didn't I?" He put his arm around his wife. "Didn't you tell them?"

"No. Since you're never here, my marital status hasn't come up." Suzy's tone was light, but her face was tense.

"Hopefully that will change with this show," Griffin said. "I've never done a show at a coffee shop, but I'll do what it takes to move to New Orleans."

Before I could tell him that Libby's café was more than a coffee shop, and he should be thankful she was helping him, Suzy did it for me.

"Griffin! Libby's café has launched the careers of many artists, so you should be grateful she agreed to host your show," Suzy snapped.

"Yes, there's no other café or any other person in the community that does as much as Libby," I said.

"Sammy's right. You're lucky Libby took your call even though you don't live here yet," Suzy said.

"Actually, it was Tessa who asked me to host the show for Griffin. She always helps her fellow artists," Libby said.

I bit my lip not to laugh as Griffin made a hasty getaway. "Ladies, please excuse me." Griffin dashed off to the bathroom again, so he didn't see Suzy shooting daggers at the back of his head.

"I should have known that he didn't contact Libby on his own." Suzy sighed. "If he can get someone else to do his dirty work, he will."

With that, Suzy flounced off and headed to the painting titled *Grits and Glory*. She stood in front of it and took out her compact from her heart-shaped purse and checked her face.

"Can you imagine not telling people about your husband? Or your wife?" Libby asked.

"Maybe they were planning to get a divorce, but now that he's moving here…"

"You don't sound convinced, Sammy." Libby raised her eyebrows. "As much as Suzy likes to gossip, I can't believe she hasn't told anyone around here about Griffin."

"Do you think Tessa knew Griffin was married?"

"I'm going to find out. If he's been leading Tessa on, this show is going to end after tonight." Libby looked over at Tessa, whose back was toward us. "Can you put the show brochures on the tables now? Thanks, honey."

I preferred to join Libby to hear what Tessa had to say about Griffin, but Libby would tell me later. Unlike Suzy, she didn't keep gossip to herself. The next person who came into the café liked gossip, too.

Winston Briggs strutted through the door. His trademark gray fedora topped his six-foot frame and covered most of his sandy-brown hair. Dressed in jeans, a white fisherman sweater, and designer tennis shoes, Winston took out his latest model cell phone.

As a self-proclaimed investigative reporter, he posted stories alluding to government corruption, shady business practices, and sordid personal affairs on his blog, *Winston's Whispers*. He'd never shown up to one of Libby's art shows, so why was he here tonight? I searched around the room looking for someone who he'd badmouthed in his blog lately, but saw no one. I'd never admit to Winston that I kept up with his blog, but I read it to learn about the latest gossip.

"Miss Libby, I'm here as a friend of the artist, not as a member of the press." Winston took off his hat and bowed when he reached Libby. "But I would be delighted if I could take a few photos to include with an interview with my old friend Griffin. If you don't mind."

"You're friends with Griffin? How do you know him?" Libby asked.

"We were all at Southern Pines University. Tessa and I were students there. Griffin was a teacher, of course, considering his age." Winston smirked. "Tessa and I haven't been as close since we graduated. Is she here tonight?"

"She is, and so is Suzy. Did you know she and Griffin were married?" Libby said.

"By your question, I'm going to guess you didn't. Tessa didn't tell you, did she?" Winston sighed. "All the girls in class had a crush on him, but he and Suzy have been married for eons. At least, legally."

"Hmm. Well, if y'all will excuse me, I need to make sure everything is ready." Libby scooted back to the bakery counter, leaving me with Winston.

"Griffin's art looks the same. I've seen worse in Jackson Square." Winston used his cell phone to snap a photo of *Moonshine Melancholy*. "Where's your boyfriend tonight, Sammy? Panhandling on Bourbon Street?"

I folded my arms and sighed. His barbs about Connor's music career annoyed me. Did Winston do this intentionally to annoy me, or did he genuinely have no respect for musicians? So far, he hadn't written anything positive or negative about the music scene in New Orleans. Considering how important music was to the city, I was surprised he hadn't. Maybe he had tried to be a musician and failed. While I was curious, I didn't have time to question him.

"I'm joking." Winston grinned, and the overhead lights highlighted the one chipped tooth in his otherwise perfect teeth. His personality was another story. He and my boyfriend, Connor, didn't hide their dislike for each other, which started when they worked at the same bar years ago. After being accused of stealing, Winston left even though he was never charged. They both had left the bar industry, but their aversion to each other still lingered.

"He's playing at Note by Note tonight, otherwise he would be here helping." I tried to keep the annoyance out of my voice. "So, what's Griffin like? I just met him briefly."

"Let me guess. He made a pass at you, or at least flirted with you? Griffin was popular with all the female students, but there was no proof he crossed the line with any of them." Winston jerked his head toward Suzy. "Either he really hasn't cheated on her or he is good at hiding his misdeeds."

"Which do you think it is?"

Winston shrugged his shoulders. "I should get to work."

Winston approached Suzy and began an animated conversation with her. Suzy shook her head until Winston left her and headed toward the bakery counter. Suzy wasn't the only one who didn't want to talk to Winston. Tessa whispered in Libby's ear and then rushed toward the kitchen. Winston stopped when he saw Tessa leave, but resumed heading that way. He took his cell phone out and interviewed Libby.

Although I found Winston irritating, Suzy and Tessa undoubtedly felt the same. Or was there more to their relationships? None of them had mentioned the others in my company.

For the next fifteen minutes, I placed plates of sweet potato scones and chocolate chip cookies on a table by the bakery counter. The table also held an urn of coffee, a hot water dispenser for tea, and bottles of sparkling water. Tessa would make lattes and other espresso drinks, but most gallery attendees drank the sparkling water or tea. Libby claimed that all the pastries would be gone.

Griffin finally came out of the restroom. He screwed the

top back on a silver flask and shoved it in his front right pocket. Clearly, he didn't really need to be concerned about the lack of alcohol because he had his own. Whether he just liked the taste or needed liquid courage, he appeared ready to mingle with the party attendees.

Either he had researched Libby's guest list, or he had a sixth sense for art collectors and gallery owners. Griffin beelined to each one and guided them to the closest painting. I eavesdropped on one conversation and stifled my laughter after he said, "Think of me as the new Southern Picasso."

Suzy pulled Griffin away after twenty minutes of this and made him sit down at the table closest to the bakery counter. "Griffin, sit down and catch your breath. If you're going to give a speech, you need to be calm, cool, and collected. Not disturbed, damp, and desperate."

"You're always looking out for me, darling." Griffin laughed and took a napkin and blotted his forehead.

"Hey, Caleb! Good to see you." Griffin stood up from the table and waved Caleb Rhodes over.

A tightness in my jaw developed as Caleb strutted over to Griffin. For the past few months, Caleb had bothered just about every business owner in the French Quarter. He first introduced himself as a new neighbor in the French Quarter. On his second visit to everyone's shop, his true identity came out; he was a real estate agent and wanted to buy or lease everyone's building. He dropped his friendly neighbor act and began pestering everyone so much so that he earned the name Caleb the Crusader.

"Hello, Caleb. I see you're friends with Griffin and Suzy." Libby approached the table with a smile I recognized as forced. When she smiled and twisted her plain gold wedding ring, it meant she was not happy.

"We're old friends from Southern Pines, Louisiana." Caleb lowered his athletic body into the chair across from Griffin. He ran a hand over his closely cropped gray hair and then straightened his blue-and-red-striped tie. So far, he was the only man wearing a tie in the café, making him stand out among the more casually dressed guests.

"Caleb is supposed to be finding the perfect gallery for Griffin here, but he seems to spend more time trying to help other people." Suzy's voice was as sweet as sugar, but the glare she gave Caleb was not.

Caleb either ignored it, was clueless, or was so used to it, he just let it roll over him. "All my clients are important to me. But Griffin knows that as one of my oldest friends, I'm looking out for him—and you, Suzy."

"How nice. If you'll excuse me, I need to say hello to a dear friend of mine." Libby scooted away to speak to a woman I knew she had just met last week. While Libby never met a stranger, the woman she ran off to wasn't someone Libby would have called a dear friend. Poor Libby must be done with this group, but the event had hours to go.

I mingled a bit, chatting with other business owners and neighbors until Libby asked me to keep an eye on the refreshment table. She had taken care of everything, leaving me with little to do. I would have been bored, but I was close to Griffin's table. They provided enough drama, especially when Winston joined them.

"The gang's all here. Who would have thought the five of us would end up in New Orleans?" Winston said.

"Five? There's four of us at the table," Caleb said.

"Didn't you know Tessa works here? She's behind the espresso machine," Suzy said. "No, you probably didn't since she doesn't own a French Quarter building."

"Oh yeah, I forgot for a second." Caleb's face turned red.

"Just like you forget you need to find a gallery for my husband? You promised you'd have a place for him to purchase by the time he finished the semester. There's only a month left," Suzy said.

"I'm trying, but Griffin's budget limits his options. He understands that," Caleb said.

"The budget is just fine, Caleb. You need to be more creative in finding me the right place," Griffin said flatly.

"Don't you have room in your shop for your husband?" Winston settled back into his chair. "If you want him here, you could make space among your T-shirts and postcards, Suzy."

Griffin reached over and clasped Suzy's hand. "Although Suzy and I are married, we have different businesses. I'm very proud of her success, and I can't wait to join her here."

"How sweet. I'll be sure to put that in my article about the show." Winston's sarcasm came through loud and clear.

"Winston, why don't you tell Griffin all about your life here? I know you have your blog, but are you dating anyone? Perhaps rekindled your romance with Tessa?" Suzy asked.

For the first time since I'd met Winston, he showed a smidgen of sadness in his eyes. He cleared his throat. "Life in New Orleans is great, thanks. Tessa and I are just friends now."

"Did you hear that, Griffin?" Suzy squeezed his hand, making him wince. "Moving here is a great opportunity for your career."

I expected her to say marriage, too, but she didn't. Then again, neither of them mentioned each other before tonight. But Suzy might have an admirer, based on Caleb's gaze. He seemed focused on Griffin, but he snuck a look at Suzy. When their eyes met, he turned away and blushed. I can't imagine why he was attracted to her, considering how much grief she gave him over not finding a gallery for Griffin. Then again, love doesn't always make sense. Suzy and Griffin's marriage was a testament to that.

Caleb switched the subject back to the show. "Your artwork looks fantastic in here, Griffin," Caleb said.

"I agree. Your new piece, *Kudzu Kinship*, fits perfectly between the two windows," Suzy said.

Suzy pointed to the artwork on the far right wall that had most of the windows. I liked that painting with its varied shades of green kudzu covering most of an old, white farmhouse. The windows of the house peeked through the invasive plant as if they were determined to hold on to its place in the world.

"Thanks, darling. It's my favorite new painting, and I'm not sure if I want to sell it." Griffin leaned over and kissed Suzy's cheek.

He turned his attention to Caleb. "Have you talked to this building's owner again about selling to me? I'd rather buy the place than lease it." Griffin surveyed the room.

"This is *my* café, Griffin." Libby's voice was as cool as her iced coffee, but her eyes were as fiery as her habanero scones.

3

"I had no idea you were interested in my café, Griffin." Libby turned toward Caleb. "Or that Caleb had spoken to my landlord. Is this the real reason for having the show here?"

"No, no, of course not. I swear on my mother's grave." Griffin did the sign of the cross. "Caleb suggested this would be a good place for me, but I didn't tell him to go see your landlord. I admit, though, after he told me about this place, I was interested. Right, Caleb? You're the one who thought of this place first."

"Um, yes. I've spoken to your landlord and many others for places for Griffin." A blotchy redness crept up Caleb's neck to his cheeks. The scowl he gave Griffin was brief but I noticed it.

"Aren't you ready to retire, Libby? I mean, you're too young, of course, but doesn't everyone want to retire sooner rather than later?" Griffin spoke in a joking manner, but I detected a serious undertone.

Libby apparently did, too. Her stony stare made me

uncomfortable, and I had done nothing. Griffin raised his eyebrows at Caleb and jerked his head toward Libby.

"Libby, I didn't mean to offend you by talking to your landlord. Don't blame Griffin for my impertinence." Caleb's tone was very measured as if he was holding back his emotions.

I didn't believe him, and I doubted Caleb believed his words either. But he was walking a tightrope, trying to be polite to Libby and protect his relationship with Griffin, who was his client.

"I came to see if any of you wanted an espresso drink before I introduce Griffin," Libby said.

"That would be fantastic, Libby. I'd love a latte, but I must have almond milk. Anything else is brutal on my stomach," Griffin said.

"Should I add that to my article, too?" Winston said.

"Yes, I'm sure your readers would love to know Griffin only drinks almond milk, annoying his wife, who hates it," Suzy said. "Libby, may I have my usual latte with nonfat milk, please?"

"I'll have the same as Suzy," Winston said.

"Me, too," Caleb said.

"I'll be back in a moment." Libby turned quickly, but I followed her.

"Libby, what's he talking about? I thought you owned the building?"

Libby kept walking, but shook her head. When we reached the counter, she said, "No, I've been renting this place for ten years now. William and I have thought about buying it, but every year I think I might retire."

"First, you're too young to retire. Second, you love this place."

Libby looked around the crowded room, filled with

happy patrons eating and drinking, looking at the artwork. "I don't know about being too young, but you're right, I love this place. I'll fight for it if I have to. Griffin is the last person I want taking over my café."

Libby went behind the counter. She spoke to Tessa, and they both stared over the espresso machine at Griffin's table. Whatever Tessa was thinking, she didn't give it away. Her face was expressionless as she made the lattes. A friend of Libby's came up to her, and she returned to her usual bubbly self.

I was relieved since I couldn't get to her after being cornered by one of the bookshop's regulars. After promising I would set aside the new Louise Penny mystery for her, she left with two cookies and a cup of mint tea. By then, Libby had returned to the table with a tray.

"I'll make my speech as you asked, and then it's your turn, Griffin." Libby placed the mug, with the blue line around the rim, to Griffin. She placed the plain white mugs in front of the other three. She put a plate of chocolate chip cookies in the middle of the table. "Please remember, the show stops at nine."

"Thank you, Libby!" Suzy said to the back of Libby's head.

"Libby is one of the nicest people in the Quarter, and you're on her bad side." Winston took two packets of sugar from the caddy and emptied them into his mug. "Not smart at all, Caleb. Or you, Griffin."

"For once, I agree with you, Winston." Suzy picked out a chocolate chip cookie from the plate and placed it on a napkin by her mug. "Libby knows everyone in the art and business community. She's not a vindictive person, but she won't do you any favors if you don't show her respect; she's earned it."

"I will be on my best behavior from now on, darling." Griffin kissed his wife on the cheek.

"Me, too." Caleb nodded as he poured cream and a packet of sugar into his latte.

Libby made her way through the tables, talking to guests as she walked. She stopped in front of *Kudzu Kinship* and raised her voice. "Good evening, y'all! Could I have your attention for a moment? Keep drinking your coffee and eating your pastries, though. Nothing should stop y'all from them."

The crowd laughed, and everyone turned their chairs to face Libby.

The four of them did the same. Suzy and Winston were positioned at the front of the table, with Griffin and Caleb seated behind them.

Libby may have intended to give a quick speech, but the crowd laughed at her jokes and shouted questions to her. She was a great storyteller, but also a beloved member of the community. I missed some of her speech to help Tessa replenish the plates of cookies and scones at the table. She didn't return to the counter, but pretended to listen to Libby. Tessa might have heard a few words, but she mainly focused on Griffin's table. Her eyes darted between all four people, which surprised me. I expected her to focus on Griffin or even Suzy. I wondered what the group dynamic was back in Southern Pines.

The four of them at the table behaved better than I expected. They didn't raise their voices, and when I wasn't helping at the table and could see them, they all appeared to be watching Libby. Their peace and quiet ended with Griffin's outburst.

He reached for his coffee, sniffed it, and put it down. "This is wrong!"

"Lower your voice, Griffin," Suzy whispered.

"This isn't my drink." Griffin leaned over Suzy's cup. "Your cup smells like almond milk. It must be mine."

"What? I don't smell almonds." Suzy tried to sniff her cup again, but Griffin took it and gave his cup to her.

"I'm sure it is." Griffin tasted the drink. "Yes, this is mine, so that's one of the nonfat lattes."

"I can't smell the difference between almond milk and regular milk," Winston said.

"Me neither. Griffin must be part bloodhound," Caleb said.

Suzy sipped her drink and made a sour face. I expected her to tell Griffin he was wrong, but she just pushed her mug away from herself.

I tried to ask Tessa if she could smell the difference between regular milk and non-dairy milks, but she had returned to the bakery counter. I turned my attention back to Libby and so did Griffin, Suzy, Caleb, and Winston.

After Libby answered one more question, "No, I am not sharing my sweet potato scone recipe with y'all. You have to be family to get it. Now, I love y'all, but I can't be momma to everyone!" After the laughter died down, Libby pulled an index card from her apron pocket.

"Tonight's artist is Griffin Blackthorn. He has been a talented artist all this life. He shares his gifts as a well-renowned professor for the past ten years at Southern Pines University. Exploring his Southern heritage through his expressive paintings is his passion." Libby paused and bit her lip. She must have been holding back her laugher like I was. "He is leaving the education field to move to New Orleans to be a full-time artist. He hopes you enjoy a slice of his world tonight." Libby shoved the card back in her pocket and pointed toward Griffin. "Welcome to the French Quarter, Griffin."

The group politely applauded, although a few giggles circulated regarding his pretentious biography. Griffin stood up and waved at the crowd. "Thank you, Libby! Let me join you up there to say a few words to my new friends, and hopefully new buyers!" He coughed. "Let me just have a sip of Libby's amazing coffee that Tessa made."

Griffin surveyed the room, and when he spotted Tessa behind the bakery counter, he grinned broadly. He took a few sips of his coffee while the crowd waited.

"Now that my throat isn't parched, let me join y'all." Griffin put his cup down and then kissed the top of Suzy's head. He started toward Libby, but only took two steps when he swayed. "Excuse me, folks, I just lost my footing for a moment."

Griffin rubbed the sides of his temples as he took a few more wobbly steps. He stopped, gripping the chair to his right. "Wow, Libby, your coffee is strong! Or did..."

Griffin turned around to face his table where Suzy, Caleb, and Winston stared at him. His face paled as he stumbled toward the table. His legs collapsed underneath him and he fell. He landed face down in between two tables. The guests scooted their chairs back, giving Griffin space on all sides.

"Griffin, are you okay?" Suzy grabbed his shoulder and shook him. "What's wrong?"

"Buddy, it was just an espresso." Caleb leaned over Winston's shoulder.

Laughter turned into an uncomfortable silence in the room.

"Let me help you up," Winston said.

Before Winston stood up to help, I rushed to Suzy and kneeled next to her. "Let's turn him on his back."

She nodded, but didn't move. I grasped Griffin's right shoulder, and with two hands, turned him on his back.

He stared at the ceiling, and his face was as white as a ghost. Griffin clenched his hands by his side as his breathing became labored.

"Griffin! Can you hear me?" I leaned over his face, trying to get his attention. But the scent of bitter almonds grabbed my attention. My years of reading cozy mysteries told me what that smell could be—cyanide.

"Griffin! What's going on? Stop playing around!" Suzy leaned in next to me to get closer to Griffin's face. "If you drank too much, I'm going to kill you..."

A loud rattling sound escaped from Griffin's lungs, and then he was silent. I placed two fingers on the hollow below his jaw, hoping to find a pulse. There was none.

Griffin was dead.

4

The noise and chaos in the café rivaled the Saints winning the Super Bowl. However, instead of a prize, there lay a lifeless man on the floor. People at nearby tables stared at Griffin, while those farther away stood up to see what was happening. Caleb bumped into their table as he rushed over to Suzy, making all the cups spill onto the tabletop. He pushed me aside to put his arm around Suzy, but she didn't notice he was there. She had a hand pressed to her mouth as she stared at her husband.

"Has someone called nine-one-one?" I yelled. Many people said yes. Debbie, a coworker of my best friend and nurse, Sissy Covington, found her way through the crowd to me.

"Let me do CPR," Debbie said.

"I'm not sure you should breathe into his mouth," I whispered in her ear. "He might have been poisoned."

She raised her eyebrows at me, but didn't react otherwise. "We only do chest compressions now for CPR."

Tessa pushed her way through the people and stopped next to Winston. "No!" she cried and stooped next to Griffin.

She reached her hand toward his face, but Winston grabbed her by the elbow.

"Tess, you can't touch him," he whispered, but she didn't respond in kind. Tessa shook her arm out of his grasp and stood up. He opened his mouth, but Tessa didn't let him speak.

"You never liked him! Stop acting like you care!" She pushed Winston with such momentum that he fell backward into the table, knocking the cups onto the floor, along with the sugar and creamer set. Suzy, Caleb, Winston, and Tessa yelled over each other, not making any sense to me and probably not to them.

I trusted my intuition that Griffin had been poisoned. Even if they were broken, the police would still need those cups. I took off my cardigan so I could grab each mug piece without directly touching them. I crouched down on the floor to locate them. There were multiple pieces of three plain white mugs and one with a blue line around the rim. They were scattered all over, along with opened and unopened yellow and pink sugar packets, and the sugar-and-creamer set. The floor was sticky with coffee and cream and rough with cookie crumbs. Sweet and bitter notes filled my nose as I searched for the cups. Just as I reached for the mug under Griffin's seat, the table jolted and I hit my head.

Rubbing my head, I scooted out from underneath the table to see Libby standing in between Caleb and Winston.

"Listen, you two, this is no time to argue. Suzy's husband is ill." Libby clutched her cell phone in both of her hands.

"She was hardly a wife," Tessa muttered as she stood near Winston.

"Oh, and you think you were more like his wife?" Suzy yelled.

Tessa and Suzy got in each other's faces, once again

bumping the table. Caleb grabbed Suzy while Winston held back Tessa. During the scuffle, someone stepped on my hand. I yelped, and only Libby noticed me over the arguing and crying.

"Sammy, what are you doing down there?" Libby reached her hand to me, and I let her help me up.

"Just trying to protect the crime...the dishes." I changed my words from the crime scene to the dishes as Libby's face went pale.

"You said crime scene, Sammy. You don't think Griffin had a heart attack?" Libby shuddered. "I told the nine-one-one operator he was having a heart attack."

"That's most likely what happened," I said, hoping I sounded confident to ease Libby's mind. "Debbie is doing CPR, and the paramedics will be here soon."

My words calmed Libby, and she took charge, making everyone, including Tessa, Suzy, Caleb, and Winston step back. Suzy wrung her hands as mascara-stained tears dripped down her face. Caleb crossed his arms as he glanced around the room. Winston tossed his cell phone from one hand to the other. Tessa rocked back and forth on her high-heel boots while coughing.

"Tessa, is your asthma bothering you? Do you have your inhaler?" Libby asked.

Libby whispered to me, "Tessa has stress-induced asthma."

If there was ever a stress-inducing situation, this was it. Tessa pulled an inhaler out of the pocket of her dress. After a few puffs, she was breathing normally. "I'm okay now."

"Remember to use it if you need it, darling." Libby put her arm around Tessa. No matter what was going on, Libby's mothering instincts were always on point.

"Has anything changed?" I asked Debbie.

She shook her head but continued doing CPR. The group remained as they were when I looked over. This time, their faces displayed the same look—fear.

"He's dead? Griffin is really dead?" Suzy rested her head in her hands as she sat at a table fifteen feet away from her husband.

"Yes, ma'am. The paramedics did all that they could for your husband." Detective Rob Armstrong pulled a chair close to Suzy and sat down. With his tall stature and muscular build, he reminded me of an adult sitting in a child's chair. His demeanor was far from immature. But he never looked as serious as his partner, Christine Gammon. Her height was accentuated in her dark, tailored suits, and her cheekbones were as sharp as her wit. Rob and Christine were the best detectives in the homicide division of the NOPD—New Orleans Police Department. They were known for their tenacity, thoroughness, and gentle approach to victims and their families.

While I was relieved to see them, I was surprised. Sure, I suspected someone poisoned Griffin, but I was no detective —as Christine always liked to remind me.

"Let me answer your question before you ask." Christine gestured for me to follow her. We avoided the broken mugs and spilled coffee and stopped two feet from Griffin's head. "Rob heard the call, but it was unclear if it was a homicide. We hoped not, for Libby's sake. And the victim's, too."

"Now that you're here, what do you think?" I rubbed my clammy hands together. If my theory was wrong, and this was a natural death, I would feel horrible taking up the detectives' time.

"Shouldn't I ask you, Nancy Drew?" Christine gave a slight smile. She was never thrilled when I appeared at a crime scene. Christine and Rob admitted my observations were worth listening to, but they preferred I didn't do more than observe.

"Call me Miss Marple, because I suspect someone poisoned Griffin with cyanide." I recounted Griffin's behavior after he drank his coffee and the odor of bitter almonds from his mouth. I shuddered as the realization hit me that a killer must be in this room. While Griffin's flirting and obvious interest in taking over Libby's cafe were loathsome, I never expected him to be killed tonight...or ever.

"He collapsed after drinking his latte..."

"Actually, it wasn't his drink at first." I looked at the smashed coffee cups. "Griffin ordered almond milk, and the others ordered nonfat milk. He started to drink his latte and said it wasn't his. He sniffed Suzy's and said it was almond milk."

"So they switched cups?" Christine took out her cell phone and made a call. "Hey, Miller, we need a crime scene team down here at Artistic Coffee and Creations. No, it's not a definitive homicide, but it's suspicious."

I couldn't deny that part of me was happy Christine took my insights seriously. But as I watched Libby twirling her wedding ring as she paced back and forth, my heart sank. A death was bad enough, but a murder was ten times worse. Of course, the situation was harder for those who cared for Griffin.

"How did Griffin know he had the wrong coffee? Almond milk doesn't have much of an odor," Christine said.

"He insisted it smelled like almond milk, but Suzy didn't. Isn't it true that some people can't smell cyanide?"

"Yes, about twenty to forty percent of the population is

missing the gene needed to detect the bitter almond odor." Christine stooped by Griffin's head. "I have that gene, and you must have it, too."

"I'd never thought I'd have to use it."

Christine stood back up. "This is going to be a long night, and it's the one time I can't ask for coffee at the scene."

By the tension in the air and the stares at the broken coffee mugs, no one appeared to want coffee tonight. If someone murdered Griffin in the café, nobody would want coffee here tomorrow...or maybe ever.

5

———

"I'll take good care of the café. I promise." Rob extended his hand.

Libby clutched the key to the café against her chest. The stress of the past few hours showed on her face. She had dark circles under eyes, wisps of hair had escaped her ponytail, and her shoulders were slumped as if she were holding up the weight of the world.

"You'll be here while they work?" Libby asked.

"Christine or I will be inside, and I promise one of us will lock up when they're done," Rob said.

Libby placed the key in Rob's hand. "I'm counting on you. Not just to take care of the café, but to find out what happened to Griffin."

"I promise I will take care of the café." Rob put the key in the breast pocket of his suit jacket. "We've got the best people working on it, Libby. I'll come by your apartment with the key tomorrow."

"Thank you. I know I can trust you and Christine." Libby exhaled, but the tension hadn't left her body.

Rob turned to Tessa who hadn't said a word for the last ten minutes. "Miss Ferguson, I'll call you tomorrow, too."

"What? I'm sorry. Can you repeat that?" Tessa rummaged in her purse for a tissue and blew her nose.

"Oh, honey. This has been so hard for you." Libby took a tissue from her own purse and wiped the tears from Tessa's face.

"I'm so sorry, Libby. You were so kind to do this show and now this happens. And now Griffin is dead." Tessa squeezed her eyes shut, but the tears kept dripping down her face.

"It's going to be all right, darling." Libby hugged Tessa. "Do you want to stay at my house tonight? You shouldn't be alone."

"My roommate is home, so I'll be fine. But thanks, Libby." Tessa gave a half-hearted smile.

"Miss Ferguson, let me have an officer drive you home," Rob said. "I'll have another one take Sammy and Libby home."

"I'd rather walk. The fresh air might do me some good. Is that okay with you, Sammy?" Libby said.

As exhausted as I felt, I didn't have the heart to say no. There was a tremor in Libby's voice that I'd never heard before. "Of course I'll walk with you. It seems we're not the only ones who need to stretch our legs."

Halfway down the block, Christine spoke with Caleb and Winston. Christine handed her card to Caleb. A police officer pulled up the police tape that surrounded the outside of the café for Caleb to walk under. A few members of the media were still hanging around, so they pounced on Caleb. He shook his head and picked up his pace, leaving the reporters behind. But when one of their own left the scene, they didn't have to chase after him.

Winston let the reporters form a circle around him. They were too far away to hear their words, but their insistent tones carried through the air. Winston didn't keep their attention for long. Christine set off toward the crowd, and they parted to let her grasp Winston's elbow. He followed her away as the reporters protested, but they switched their attention to the crime scene investigators who carried around numerous evidence bags.

"I was just reminding Winston that we prefer that the details of tonight are kept to yourselves," Christine said in a no-nonsense voice.

"Freedom of the press..."

Christine's hand shot up as if she were stopping traffic. "Yes, I understand about freedom of the press. Just as you understand that it's important that tonight's tragedy doesn't become sensationalized. We have to investigate, and as you said yourself, Griffin was a friend of yours."

Tessa snorted when Christine said friend. Winston took offense.

"We were friends, at least back in the day. Maybe we would have been friends when he moved here." Winston took off his hat and ran a hand through his hair. "I'll write about Griffin's death as a reporter and not from my personal viewpoint."

"Then we understand each other." Christine offered her hand to Winston. "We'll be in touch for a formal witness statement from you, but call me or Rob in the meantime with any questions."

Winston hesitated but he shook Christine's hand. "Thank you, Detective. Tessa, can I escort you home?"

"No." Tessa shook her head. "No, thank you. A police officer is taking me. Detective Armstrong, can I go now, please?"

Rob waved over an officer and instructed him to drive Tessa home. Winston tried to finagle a ride with them, but Tessa said they lived in opposite directions. Whether that was true or not, Tessa didn't give Winston an opportunity to challenge her. She dashed to the police car with the officer.

"Give her a little time, Winston." Libby put her hand on Winston's arm. "She'll need a friend sooner rather than later."

"I'm not sure if I'll be the friend she'll want." Winston sighed. "But I'll be around if she needs me. Tell her that for me, Libby."

"I will," Libby promised.

"I'm going to go if there's nothing else, Detectives," Winston said. "Unless I can offer to walk Libby and Sammy home."

While I wanted to ask Winston questions about his relationships with everyone from Southern Pines and what he saw at the table, I declined. Libby shook her head ever so slightly at his offer, so I wanted to respect her wishes. And I guessed that Winston's overture wasn't one of chivalry, but one of interrogating Libby and me about tonight. He would have to wait just like I would for any exchange of information.

Another reason I didn't want him around was Connor was on his way to walk us home. He'd heard the news during a set break and was rushing over to the café now. He texted, *Heard the news about a death at the café. Tell Momma I'm on my way. Please don't tell me it's murder.* I sent a thumbs-up emoji since I couldn't tell him it wasn't murder.

Libby's husband, William, was out of town, otherwise he would have come over, too. Thank goodness Connor wasn't traveling tonight, as Libby would need all the support she could get. Not that me and all her other friends wouldn't be there for her, but her husband and son were her biggest supporters in the world.

Connor and Winston didn't get along, and I didn't want to hear their verbal sparring tonight. As I watched Winston leave the area, with his hat clenched in his hands and his shoulders drooped, I wondered if he would have even said one snide comment to Connor. Tonight seemed to have affected Winston more than I imagined. As Libby and I huddled together in the chilly night air, I reflected on not just how tonight affected Winston, but also Tessa, Caleb, and of course, Suzy. What were they really feeling— sadness, fear, or guilt?

Tonight I needed to get Libby home and settled, but tomorrow I'd look into those four people. I had no choice. As Griffin's body was removed from the café, light bulbs lit up the street as they snapped photo after photo. Libby stifled a sob, but a tear rolled down her cheek as I shielded her from the press.

The coroner escorted Suzy out of the café and guided her to a police car. Suzy wore her cat's-eye sunglasses, but it didn't hide all the redness around her eyes. The coroner closed the door, gave two knocks on the roof, and the car left, following the van with Griffin's body.

Libby left my embrace to stare at the van with Griffin and the car with Suzy leave the street. Libby cared for everyone in the community, so there was no doubt she was hurting for Suzy. But Libby was also a practical business-woman, and she knew how horrible this situation would be for her business. Even if Griffin wasn't murdered, the death would haunt Libby and the café until the truth was revealed.

6

———

When I opened my door at 6:22 a.m., I expected it would be one of my neighbors checking in on me. We had a group text for Thibodeaux Mansion, and I messaged the group to explain what had happened. Everyone was a part of it, including my next door neighbor, Ruby Virtue, although she never responded or commented on anything. But she definitely read the texts.

"Ruby, what are you doing knocking at my door at this hour? Didn't the spirits tell you I had a long night?" I tightened the belt on my fluffy robe as I shivered from the early morning air. Nubi, my cat, threaded in and out of my legs and meowed. "See, even Nubi thinks it's too early for cats, humans, and spirits."

The wrinkles on Ruby's face deepened as she frowned at me. "There are so many things wrong with your ramblings. First, the spirits have not spoken about you this morning. Second, I turn off my phone at night as the electronic energy disrupts my sleep. I just read about the horrible incident at Libby's café. How is she? Is she home?"

I stared at Ruby as my sleep-and coffee-deprived brain

tried to comprehend what she asked. Was she really concerned about Libby? Over the past few months, Ruby had participated in a few of our gatherings in the courtyard, but she still kept to herself most of the time. And while we had a better understanding of each other after I helped her with the disappearance and reappearance of her daughter, Verity, we still weren't the best of friends.

While I cleared her daughter's name in a murder case, it was Libby who provided emotional support. Everyone at Thibodeaux Mansion was shocked that she let Libby into her apartment and into her world. Perhaps Ruby wanted to return the favor.

She did.

"Libby absorbs emotions like a sponge so she must be beside herself. A corpse in the café is not good for her mind, body, soul, and business." Ruby took a black stone out of the pocket of her long, silk emerald-green dress. A scarf in a matching color held back her silver hair, and I noted the scent of her jasmine perfume. Ruby was dressed for the day which was unusual. She must really be worried about Libby.

While I can't say that I believed all of Ruby's ideology, I was worried about Libby, too. Last night when Connor met us at the café, she calmly explained what happened to Griffin. It wasn't until we reached her apartment that she broke down completely. All her sadness, stress, and fears spilled out in a cascade of tears. Connor stayed with her to make sure she slept. I had assured Connor I'd be all right by myself and returned to my apartment.

"On that, we agree. I can text Connor to see if she's up—"

Ruby put her hands up like a crossing guard, stopping traffic. "I'm receiving a message. Anna says that Libby is awake. I'll go see her now."

"Hold it. Who's Anna?" I had to step around Nubi, who was lying on the slate tiles with Ruby's cats, Cleopatra and Nefertiti. The cold tiles made my feet ache, so I couldn't imagine how the cats could be comfortable laying there.

"She is the spirit of a young lady who lived in the mansion decades ago. Anna is fond of Libby and spends much of her time in Libby's apartment," Ruby said matter-of-factly. "Apparently, Anna hasn't visited you. No surprise there, as she prefers to avoid those who bring trouble to the physical and spiritual world."

"Well then, I guess I won't invite her in for coffee." My sarcasm was partly due to my exhaustion from last night but also from Ruby's constant remark equating me to trouble. Sure I had been involved in a few mysteries and murders since becoming her neighbor, but otherwise I was a considerate neighbor.

"I doubt she would accept, but you might ask Ronald if he'd like a cup." Ruby pointed to the water fountain in the back of the courtyard. Instead of water, plants filled each tier, spilling down upon each other. "He only appears now and then, but he likes coffee."

Ruby gathered the hem of her dress and started toward the door that led into the main building that housed Libby and William's apartment. Cleopatra and Nefertiti followed her, their black fur glistening in the rising sun. I half expected Nubi to follow them, but he trotted back into our apartment.

Just as I turned to join him, there was a rustling in the water fountain. Normally I would have chalked it up to the cats since it was one of their favorite hiding spots. But they weren't there. Of course, another neighborhood cat or bird might be making themselves at home among the lush plants. But I just had to be a smart aleck. "Ronald, you'll have to be quiet if you want coffee this early."

The noise grew louder, and I shivered as if a breeze had blown through the courtyard. But it had not. Suddenly the movement stopped, and Ruby's laughter broke the silence.

She stood in the doorway with her arms crossed and a smirk on her face. "If you're going to believe in the spirits, you're going to have to be nicer than that, Samantha. That is if there is a Ronald who frequents the courtyard."

Ruby went into the building, shutting the door behind her. It was too early for this. But as I went to close my apartment door, I swore I heard the sound of someone stirring a spoon in a coffee mug. Now I was just letting Ruby get into my head. Or it could have been the events of last evening running through my mind. Last night, and now this morning, was full of surprises. I wondered what waited for me at work today.

7

─────────

"Andrew, I picked up breakfast... Suzy?" I almost dropped the bag of beignets and the tray holding two cups of café au lait when I entered Lagniappe Books. When I texted Andrew Ballard, one of my closest friends and business partner, this morning, he didn't mention Suzy was at the shop.

"Here, let me help you with that, Samantha." Andrew left Suzy in the sitting area at the back of the shop.

Suzy looked the part of a 1950s' housewife in mourning. Her simple black dress fitted her curves and fell just below her knees. She wore a strand of pearls and a simple gold wedding band I had never seen her wear before. A pair of large, black sunglasses sat on the coffee table, along with her black patent-leather purse.

I placed the coffee and beignets on the long dining room table that served as a display for recently released books and as our sales desk. Mahogany shelves filled with books from every genre lined the walls. Customers would roam from bookshelf to bookshelf, often picking up a book and taking it to the seating area in the rear of the store. The plush burgundy love seat, along with two matching chairs and a stylish marble coffee table, made the space feel like a home library instead of a store.

He took the bag of beignets and whispered, "Suzy was yelling at a reporter outside her shop when I arrived. I couldn't leave her alone, so I sent the reporter on his way and brought her here."

Andrew wasn't an imposing man with his trademark red bow tie, white oxford shirt, and tan dress pants. But his serious face and short salt-and-pepper hair gave him an air of authority that worked on most people. He had his own negative experiences with the media, so I imagined he succinctly told the reporter to move on.

"She was at her store? The day after her husband died?" I whispered as we walked toward the back. At least I thought I whispered.

"It must seem absurd that I went to my shop, but I didn't know what else to do. There's no handbook for young widows, is there?" Suzy tore the tissue in her hands. "The police haven't told me anything. The coroner says they don't know when they'll release his body, so I can't plan a funeral. I'm so lost today."

My cheeks burned from embarrassment. Everyone responds to tragedy differently, and I shouldn't have judged Suzy for coming to her store. I sat on the sofa next to her. "I'm sorry, Suzy. That was insensitive of me. You should go or do whatever you need to do today."

I managed to put the coffees on the table before Suzy threw her arms around me. "I knew you would understand. My house felt so empty this morning. I couldn't stay there."

Suzy finished hugging me and leaned back against the sofa. Her eyes were watery, but no tears had fallen down her flawlessly made-up face. Again, I shouldn't be critical, as getting dressed and putting on makeup were just part of the motions of getting ready in the morning. But I couldn't help but ask about one thing she said.

"Suzy, did Griffin visit New Orleans often?"

"No. Why do you ask?" Suzy sat up straight and twisted her wedding ring.

"It's just you mentioned the house felt empty this morning, so I assumed Griffin was in town often," I said. "I'm sorry we didn't meet him before last night."

"With his teaching schedule, he didn't visit often. When he did, it was usually for a night and then he was gone. A year of being in two cities turned into three before we knew it."

"I remember when you opened your shop." Andrew sat down across from us. "You impressed me with your ability to work on your own. I never saw your husband helping you. I assume you would have introduced us if he had."

"No, he didn't help me." Suzy gripped the arm of the sofa.

"Is that why you've never mentioned him? I don't mean to be rude, but I find it strange you never told us you were married." Andrew used a voice I called his professor voice. He spoke firmly, but with a hint of compassion. I imagined he used it with failing students.

"Oh, you know, it just didn't come up." Suzy stared at the floor.

"Come on now. You're among friends here." Andrew pushed the box of tissues closer to her.

"I was so embarrassed. I *am* so embarrassed." Suzy raised her head as the tears trickled down her face. "When I moved here to open the shop, our marriage was rocky. We were supposed to move together to New Orleans, but Griffin didn't get the job at Tulane. I made the move, but Griffin was…"

I handed a tissue to Suzy. "Griffin was jealous?"

"No, he was disappointed. He always wanted the best for me, but being trapped in Southern Pines was tough for him," Suzy said. "The shop keeps me busy and his students kept him busy. Girls like Tessa pounced on him as soon as I left town. Poor Griffin had to bat them off like flies on a cow patty."

Andrew and I exchanged confused glances. Did she compare the female students to flies and her husband to a cow patty? She definitely needed a widow's manual to understand that calling your husband cow poop wasn't appropriate.

"Since I've been teaching at Tulane, I have seen students become enamored with their professors. Fortunately, most keep their relationships professional with their students." Andrew was being polite, but Suzy got the point.

"No, he didn't have affairs with them." Suzy shook her head. "Yes, I know Tessa had a crush on him when she was a student. Based on her behavior last night, it seems she still does."

"You were surprised, weren't you, that she had arranged the show for Griffin?" I said.

"Yes! I mean, I'm at Libby's once or twice a week. You'd think Tessa would have said something to me." Suzy stuck her nose in the air. "But then again, she tries to avoid me. I can't imagine why. I'm always nice to her."

Suzy's treatment of Tessa made me question her sincerity. Suzy wasn't the only person Tessa was unhappy to see last night.

"Tessa didn't want to talk to Winston, either, last night," I said. "She was very busy helping Libby."

"Maybe, but I'm not surprised she avoided Winston." Suzy's shoulders relaxed. "Tessa and Winston dated in college but broke up before they finished. I don't think Winston ever got over her. It's funny how they both ended up in New Orleans."

"It seems like people from Southern Pines like to move to New Orleans. There's you, Tessa, Winston, and Caleb already here," I said.

"Griffin is finally here, but in the morgue." Suzy wailed and drooped over the side of the sofa.

"Now, now. You'll make it through this. I promise," Andrew said, gesturing for me to stand so he could take my spot on the sofa. "I won't lie and say it'll be easy. You need to use all your inner strength but also learn to lean on those that love you."

I grabbed a bottle of water from the mini-fridge in our office as Andrew spoke to Suzy. Andrew lost his partner during Hurricane Katrina, and his death still haunted him. But as he told Suzy, he learned to lean on his loved ones over the years. When he met someone who suffered a loss like himself, Andrew shared his story to offer them hope. The tragic death of my cousin Jasper St. Martin's girlfriend recently meant Andrew and Jasper spoke often. Andrew's kindness is one thing I loved about him.

After giving them a few minutes to themselves, I rejoined them. "Would you like a bottle of water, Suzy? I could make tea if you prefer."

Suzy finished wiping her eyes and shoved the tissue in the pocket of her dress. Despite her tears, her mascara remained perfect. She must wear industrial-strength makeup. Was Suzy's grief authentic or an act?

Andrew cleared his throat. "Samantha, can you get Suzy a cup of chamomile tea now?"

"What? I'm sorry. My mind was off somewhere else." I must have missed a part of the conversation. "Let me get that for you."

"No, thank you. I'm okay now. I should put a sign on the shop that I'll be closed for a while." Suzy stood up and smoothed her dress down. "Thank you both for listening."

"We are here for you, Suzy." Andrew put his arm around Suzy and walked her to the door. "You are welcome here or you can call us anytime."

"Yes, let us know what we can do to help." I joined them at the front door.

"Y'all are so kind." Suzy kissed us each on the cheek. "If you hear anything about Griffin's murder, you'll let me know, won't you?"

"O-of course," I stammered. Why did Suzy say murder? Nowhere in the media did it say Griffin's death had been declared a homicide. She had said earlier the police had told her nothing. Had she overheard my conversation with Christine last night? Or had she come to her own conclusion? If she poisoned him, then this could have been a slip of the tongue.

Andrew opened the door, and Suzy cautiously descended the steps and stood on the sidewalk. As Andrew locked the door, I rushed over to the front window. I pretended to arrange the books and the new Thanksgiving decorations. The artist who made our Halloween bat decorations from old pages of damaged books made turkeys for us. Along with fake maple leaves, the display set the mood for the fall.

"You're spying on Suzy, aren't you?" Andrew fixed the perfectly neat stack of books next to me.

"Like you aren't?" I softly nudged him. "What do you

make of her? You talked to her more than I did. Is she really mourning Griffin's death?"

"Yes, I believe she's bereft. But then again, many killers mourn the loved ones they have killed."

"I agree with you, Professor."

Andrew shook his head. "I'm a historian, not a psychologist. But we both have known remorseful murders."

"You're right." I bit the inside of my lip so I wouldn't cry. Both Andrew and I had loved ones who turned out to be murderers. Even their sense of remorse didn't make the reality of their crimes easier to bear.

"I'm not sure if Suzy had something to do with Griffin's death, but I'm going to keep an eye on her."

"Because most people are killed by someone they know?" Andrew asked. "And she sat next to her husband before he died?"

"Yes, and yes. But also, did you notice she called Griffin's death a murder? The police haven't said officially that it was murder." I watched Suzy wave off a reporter from her doorstep. "Does Suzy know more than she's saying?"

8

"Now you girls go out for your run. I'm fine." Libby kissed me on the cheek. "Connor is taking good care of me until William comes home tonight."

"Are you sure? You look a little pale." Sissy Covington grasped Libby's hands after she kissed her on the cheek.

"Always the nurse. Aren't you?" Libby squeezed Sissy's hands. "I admit I didn't get much sleep. My mind wouldn't stop thinking about poor Griffin."

I tried to talk to Libby all day, but she never responded. Connor did, otherwise I would have been at Libby's front door earlier. Connor had been with his mom since we returned home last night. He texted me throughout the day to give me updates on his mom and to check on me. I was tired, too, but nothing like Libby. Her red eyes, slumped shoulders, and pale skin made it clear she was exhausted and stressed.

Connor came down the apartment hallway to stand behind his mom. He twirled the mouthpiece to his trumpet, which was his nervous tic. While he had a smile on his handsome face, his brown eyes betrayed his anxiety. He wrapped his arms around her shoulders and rested his head on top of hers. "I've tried to get her to rest, but Momma is either pacing or on the phone. Sissy as a medical professional, can you tell her to eat and get some sleep?"

"Libby, as a nurse, your tenant, and as your friend, listen to your son. Rob and Christine are working day and night on this."

"And you, too, Sammy?" Libby took her hands from Sissy.

Connor and Sissy grinned at each other. They enjoyed calling out my detective skills when it came to situations in the Quarter. Others called it being nosy. Rob and Christine called it interfering. Well, only sometimes, since I shared what I learned. I did that earlier today, relaying Andrew and my chat with Suzy. Rob thanked me for calling with the information, but didn't give me anything in return.

"I'm sure Rob and Christine will figure out what happened to Griffin." I hugged Libby. "When can you get back into the café?"

"Tomorrow." Libby's voice had all the enthusiasm of someone getting ready for a root canal without anesthesia.

"I've arranged for a professional crew to clean the entire café. They couldn't squeeze us in until tomorrow, though," Connor said.

"It doesn't matter when they show up. I don't know when I'll reopen." Libby turned and took three steps down the hall. "If I even reopen."

Connor, Sissy, and I protested, but Libby didn't turn around. She shuffled down the hall and entered the powder room, closing the door behind her, shutting out any conversation.

"Momma isn't herself. Last night might be the last straw,

though, when it comes to the café." Connor sighed. "So she is worried about her lease?" I asked.

"More than she's letting on, according to my dad." Connor kissed me. "Y'all should go for your run. Sammy, I'll call you later. Sissy, if Rob lets anything slip..."

"I'll let you know. I promise." Sissy squeezed his arm. Connor closed the door, and Sissy and I went to the courtyard.

"Let's stretch quickly so we can go run." Sissy bent over to touch her toes. "You need to fill me in on all the details of last night."

Sissy wore purple running pants and a matching Louisiana State University sweatshirt. To finish her look, Sissy wore purple sneakers and pulled back her blonde hair with a purple scrunchie. Wearing scrubs for her job meant she wore colorful clothing when she wasn't at the hospital. My standard running outfit consisted of plain black leggings, a black long-sleeve T-shirt, and whatever ponytail holder Nubi hadn't taken as a toy that I could find.

We stretched quickly and jogged out of the courtyard toward Royal Street. For a few hours during the day, the street was closed to vehicles. It was open to cars now, so we maneuvered around clumps of pedestrians on the sidewalk. We came upon the biggest crowd at the corner of Governor Nicholls Street.

Sissy slowed down after leading me through a tour group milling around the LaLaurie Mansion. Named as one of the most haunted homes in New Orleans, every tour group stopped here, day or night. The Italianate-style mansion was three stories tall with a wrought-iron balcony that went around the entire second floor. Being privately owned, no tours were allowed inside, yet that didn't prevent people from stopping to gaze and search for ghosts.

"Do you think that place is haunted?" I asked when we were out of earshot of the group. "Neal believes it's an unlucky spot, but doesn't think it's haunted."

"Neal is one of the most pragmatic tour guides in the Quarter." Sissy laughed. Our friend and neighbor, Neal Bennett, owned New Orleans Past & Present Tours. He focused on the history and architecture of the city. But his lack of belief in ghosts and vampires didn't keep him from sharing stories about New Orleans supernatural lore.

"He is the best and most truthful tour guide. I wonder if half the guides even tell people that this isn't the original building the LaLaurie family lived in when the fire broke out."

I'd taken many tours with Neal, and he prided himself on sharing facts, not just rumors or lore. A fire revealed that Madame LaLaurie and her husband had tortured and murdered their slaves. The fire not only destroyed the building, but the lives of the family in New Orleans. They left the country, and the property was rebuilt and used as a girls' school, boarding house, and eventually became a private residence again.

"I don't know if it's haunted, but I do feel nauseous when I walk by it." Sissy shuddered. "Madame LaLaurie was an evil woman, and the people she hurt and killed would have every right to haunt the place."

"I hope Griffin doesn't haunt Libby's café." This time, I shuddered.

We turned left on Governor Nicholls, and once we were past another tour group heading to the mansion, we stopped running. I didn't want to raise my voice as I recounted last night, so we walked. By the time we reached Rampart Street, Sissy knew everything.

"You really think Griffin was poisoned?" Sissy said.

"I do. Has Rob said anything to you?"

Sissy frowned. "Nothing. He and Christine are still in charge, though, so I'd say they believe he was poisoned, too."

I imagined it was hard enough to investigate crimes in your own neighborhood. But the worst part must be having your fiancée bothering you for information. I'd witnessed Sissy's demands to Rob, and she was a tough cookie. But Rob held his own.

"Of all the people who were there, who's your prime suspect? Libby is off the list, right?" Sissy said. "And not just because she's your boyfriend's momma?"

"I can't imagine Libby killing anyone, even if they were trying to steal her café. But could this have been someone's way of getting Libby to leave? Griffin or Suzy might not have even been the targets."

"From what you've told me about Griffin, he seems to have been ripe for the picking," Sissy said.

"True, but what if Suzy was the target? The only two people who might have motives are Griffin and Tessa. Unless there's more to the relationships of that group." I stumbled on a crack on the sidewalk. My mind wasn't on the run now, but all the information I was missing.

Sissy grabbed me before I fell to the ground. "Let's change plans and not run through Armstrong Park."

"I just stumbled. We don't have to stop running because of me."

"I know, but we need burgers to continue our conversations. Let's head over to Port of Call."

The restaurant was our favorite for big, juicy cheeseburgers served only with baked potatoes with all the fixings. I also liked all their fruity drinks, but I learned quickly that one was enough. Even deceptively weak cocktails in New Orleans are actually strong.

"If I was a good friend, I'd say no." I hadn't run for a few days, so I needed the exercise. But my heart wasn't really in it, so I didn't argue too much.

"Yeah! Dinner is on me since I dragged you away from your workout," Sissy said.

"Besides talking about Griffin's death, we can talk about your meeting with the latest wedding planner."

Sissy groaned. "I'd rather talk about murder. The wedding planner my momma's friend recommended is a definite no."

"What did this one suggest?"

So far, Sissy and her mother had met with two other planners. The first only did destination weddings in the Caribbean, and there was no way Rob and Sissy weren't getting married in New Orleans. Rob had arrested the second planner's third cousin for manslaughter. Not only was it an awkward situation, but the woman told Sissy she'd give her a discount if Rob put in a good word at her cousin's parole hearing.

"This one's big idea was a Christmas-theme wedding. We'd have a snow machine cover Jackson Square where a reindeer-driven sleigh would deliver me to St. Louis Cathedral."

Sissy's face was as sour as a bitter lemon. I tried to keep my composure, but I burst out laughing. "At least she didn't suggest dressing up as Santa and Mrs. Claus."

"I didn't give her the chance." Sissy rolled her eyes. "I told my momma we weren't talking to any wedding coordinators that are cousins or friends of our family or friends."

"Darn, I was going to ask if you wanted Aunt Charlene to help."

"She'd be better than the ones I've met. At least your aunt would be fun to work with, although I might not get a word in edgewise."

Sissy was right about not getting to talk. Charlene St. Martin was a chatty woman about any and all subjects. As the sister-in-law of my biological father, she and her son, Jasper, were my only living blood relatives. Aunt Charlene could be as loud and bold as her floral dresses. The only thing bigger than the white leather purse she carried was her love of her family and friends.

"If you don't mind having blush and bashful as your wedding colors, she's your woman."

"I do like pink." Sissy's laugh erased the stress on her face. "Come on, let's order pink drinks with our burgers."

"You are a bad influence."

"Don't you know it!" Sissy threaded her arm through mine and steered me toward Port of Call. We were heading down Rampart Street to Esplanade Avenue when I grabbed Sissy's arm.

"Sissy, don't look, but Suzy is walking across the street." From the corner of my eye, I recognized Suzy's black dress from earlier. And I recognized the man with her... Caleb.

9

Caleb and Suzy crossed Rampart Street and headed down Barracks Street. Caleb carried a grocery bag from a small organic foods grocery store. Although the sunlight was fading, Suzy wore sunglasses.

"Come on!" I waited for two cars to pass, then I rushed across the street. Sissy followed me without question. We were about twenty-five feet behind Caleb and Suzy, with five people in between us.

"Who's that with Suzy?" Sissy asked.

"It's Caleb Rhodes, the real estate developer."

"That's a strange pair, considering what you told me about them from last night."

"What's even stranger is that they seem very comfortable with each other."

Caleb and Suzy walked shoulder to shoulder with their heads turned toward each other. From their profiles, their faces appeared relaxed as they spoke to one another. As they reached the next corner, Caleb placed his hand near the small of Suzy's back as they stepped down into the street.

Even though he hadn't touched her, the gesture was something a close friend or romantic partner would make.

Before we reached the next corner, four of the group who were walking in between us and Caleb and Suzy entered a bar. It left just one person in between us, a man I hadn't paid attention to before.

"I can't believe I didn't see him earlier," I whispered to Sissy. "He's not wearing his hat."

"Who? Oh my goodness, is that Winston?" Sissy grabbed my arm as she stopped, making me jerk backward.

"Shhh! Keep your voice down! Let's keep going."

Winston must not have heard us since he kept walking ten feet behind them. We kept our pace fifteen feet behind him. After crossing one more block, Caleb and Suzy stopped in front of a blue shotgun cottage. Suzy reached into her purse and pulled out a set of keys, and hopped up to her door. Caleb placed a foot on the first step, but didn't go any farther. Suzy's hand was up like a traffic cop and Caleb got the hint.

"Suzy must be done with Caleb tonight," Sissy said from our spot by a streetlight. We stooped, pretending to tie our shoes.

"It looks like Caleb would have been happy to keep talking with Suzy. I wish I knew what about."

"Do you want to knock on her door when Caleb leaves? We can say we were checking in on her since we were running by her house," Sissy said.

I laughed softly. "Are you suggesting that because you have good Southern manners or because you're a good amateur detective?"

"If Rob asks, it's my Southern manners." Sissy grinned. "But everyone else knows you're a bad influence on me."

"I resent that remark." I feigned indignation.

"No, honey, you resemble that remark."

Caleb handed the grocery bag to Suzy, and she left him on the doorstep. He waited until her door closed and then took out his cell phone. As he made a call, he continued down Barracks Street and then made a right onto Royal Street.

"Let's go." Sissy went to stand up, but I pulled her back down.

"Wait. Winston is going to the door."

Winston had the same idea as us, apparently, and trotted to Suzy's door. I motioned for Sissy to follow me into the street. We stooped behind a yellow Volkswagen bug parked in front of Suzy's house. We craned our necks around the front end of the car so we could hear them.

"Winston, I'm in no mood to talk to you. Please go away." Suzy had her arms crossed and a deep frown on her face as she blocked her doorway.

"Suzy, I'm not here as a reporter. Honestly, I'm here as Griffin's friend, as your friend." Winston put his hand over his heart.

"Oh, please. You weren't his friend." Suzy shook her head. "And in the three years I've been in New Orleans, you've only talked to me when you've wanted something for your blog. That's not friendship."

"Suzy..." Winston pleaded, but Suzy slammed the door in Winston's face. He rushed down the stairs and stomped off in the direction Caleb had gone.

"Do you want to follow him, or do you want to go see Suzy?" Sissy asked.

"I don't think Suzy would welcome us after watching her reaction to Winston," I said.

"How about Winston, though? He might be going to talk to Caleb."

"True, but I want to talk to Caleb without Winston. I have a feeling no one is going to talk comfortably around Winston. No one wants their words in one of his articles."

"Ain't that the truth?" Sissy laughed.

I put my hands on the car to stand up and immediately regretted it. My hands were covered in dust. Finding a parking space in the French Quarter was always difficult, so many people didn't move their car until they absolutely needed to use it. By the dirt coating my hand, this car hadn't been moved in ages.

"Oh, I'm a mess now." I wiped my hands on my running pants, but it didn't help much.

"*Tsk, tsk*. Don't you know not to touch a car in the Quarter? Either an alarm is going to go off or you'll end up filthy." Sissy stretched her arms above her head. "Since you're all dirty and all this detecting has made me tired, I don't want to go to Port of Call after all. Let's grab takeout from Frankie's and eat on your couch. We can watch an Agatha Christie movie and brush up on our detection skills."

"What do you mean, brush up on our detection skills? We're pretty good at it, aren't we?" I laughed as we headed toward Frankie's Groceries.

No, our detection skills were not as good as I thought.

The gate to Thibodeaux Mansion was slightly ajar when we arrived. I didn't think much of it as it didn't lock. Now and then, Libby and William would poll the residents to see if we wanted the lock fixed. The group consensus was no since so many guests and delivery drivers came in through the courtyard gate. But after finding one of my least favorite people sitting at my bistro table, I might change my mind.

I almost dropped my bag at the sight of Winston sitting at my table outside my apartment. His feet rested on the table as he leaned back in the chair. I clutched my grocery bag tighter and took in a deep breath to calm myself. My first inclination was to yell at him, but I used those Southern manners Sissy mentioned earlier.

"Winston, if I knew you were waiting, I would have brought dinner for you, too." I put my bag on the other chair and faced him with a fake smile.

"Really? You would have brought me dinner?" Winston swung his feet off the table and stood up. "What would Connor say?"

"He would have told you to get your grubby feet off that table." Sissy stood on her tiptoes and got as close as she could to Winston's face. She refrained from using her Southern manners. "Didn't your momma tell you it's not polite to show up to a lady's house, uninvited?"

"Didn't your momma tell you not to follow people around?" Winston stepped backward with a smirk on his face. "I caught you two following me on Barracks. You could have said hi instead of following me around like schoolgirls with a crush."

"Oh, you wish." Sissy rolled her eyes. "We were out on a run this evening. If we crossed paths, it was just a coincidence."

"Actually, we were following Caleb and Suzy." I put my hand on Sissy's arm so she'd stop ranting. "Like you, Winston."

"So you admit you were following me?" Winston put his fingers together in a steeple shape like he was a villain who had won a battle.

"No, we were following Caleb and Suzy. I didn't even notice you until we reached Suzy's block. You're not wearing your fedora," I snapped. I was done pretending to be nice. "You didn't have it on so they wouldn't notice, right?"

"I don't always wear it." Winston ran a hand through his sandy-brown hair. "All right, let's agree that all of us were following them. What did you think?"

"You tell me. You're friends with them," I said.

Sissy snorted.

"I take it you heard Suzy." Winston frowned at Sissy.

"We did. Was it true?" Sissy scowled back at him.

"No. I've tried to be her friend since she moved here. All she cared about was getting her shop up and running and begging Griffin to move here."

"Sounds like you knew Griffin well since you went to Southern Pines University. So you considered yourself his and Suzy's friend?" I said.

"Yes. And I'm friends with Caleb and Tessa, too."

"Caleb seems to be closer to Suzy than you," I said.

"Sure, I mean, they're closer in age." Winston smiled, but it seemed forced. "He just beat me to the punch and offered to help her. Did you notice the grocery bag?"

"We did. Do you think she called him for help, or did he show up uninvited?" Sissy interjected. "If you had gotten to her first, would she have let you help her?"

"Is this an interrogation? Isn't that her boyfriend's job?" Winston glared at Sissy.

"He's my fiancé, and yes, he's investigating Griffin's death." Sissy put her bag on the table and then put her hands on her hips.

"Congratulations." Winston's sarcasm was as thick as Sissy's Southern accent. "But it seems like you and Sammy are also investigating. How about it, Sammy?"

Winston winked and grinned, a routine I imagined worked on many women. He was attractive, I'd give him that, but I'd never let him know. I didn't respond to his actions with a smile, but kept my face like the *Mona Lisa*.

"I'm just checking in on people. Suzy and Libby are my friends and that's what friends do," I said.

"Sure, sure, I get that. But come on." Winston stepped closer to me and leaned down into my face. "You want to find the killer as much as I do. But I'll solve this before you do. Wanna make a bet?"

"We're helping Libby. You only want page reads for your blog." Sissy stepped in between Winston and me.

Winston backed away. "I'm a reporter. That's what I do, and there's nothing wrong with that."

He started toward the courtyard exit, but halfway there, he turned around. "Oh, in case you're wondering, I had nothing to do with Griffin's murder. I'm one less suspect for you."

The next door neighbor began playing a slow jazz number on his clarinet. Winston must have taken it as a sign to leave, as he scowled at us before stomping off. The gate clattered loudly just as the clarinet hit a long, high note.

"He is a piece of work. Did he think he could flirt with you to get you to help him?" Sissy grumbled as she picked up her bag.

"I think he flirts with everyone, hoping to get what he wants." I took my keys out of my pants pocket and grabbed my groceries. "But it doesn't work on me. I won't help him, nor am I taking him off my suspect list. Investigating a murder you committed would be the perfect way to take suspicion off yourself."

10

I woke up this morning even more determined to find Griffin's killer. Winston's visit last night lit a fire under me. Of course I wanted to solve the mystery for Libby's sake, but I had to admit Winston got under my skin. Sissy tried to convince me I shouldn't have been embarrassed that Winston knew we were following Caleb and Suzy.

"We aren't real detectives, so I'd say we did pretty good last night," Sissy had said. "Winston just wants attention, and he'll do whatever he can to get it."

Yes, my ego was bruised, but Winston's cocky attitude and his offer to turn this situation into a bet made me mad. The murder affected so many people including him if he was really the friend of Griffin's he claimed to be. There was no way I was taking him off my suspect list. I doubted I'd get much information from Winston, but hopefully those who knew him would tell me what I needed to know.

"Nubi, what are your plans today?" I made coffee and then joined my cat on the love seat where he washed his face with his paws. For all the roaming Nubi did with Ruby's cats, he was always immaculate. I rubbed the little white spot of fur on the top of his head.

"Meow. Meow."

"Oh, you're staying in today? Good idea. The weather is chilly." I put my coffee mug down and showed Nubi the weather report on my cell phone as if he could read it. Didn't all cat parents do this—talk to their cats as if they could understand them? The way Nubi would comfort me when I was upset or meow joyfully when I laughed made me think he understood me.

A knock at my door caused both of us to jump. Nubi didn't move, but I tightened my robe and checked the peephole. I swung the door open.

"Good morning, y'all. Did you want some coffee?" I asked Connor, Libby, and William, who stood outside my door. I cringed as I realized offering coffee probably wasn't the best idea under the recent circumstances. Fortunately, they didn't notice my faux pas. By the looks on their faces, I wasn't sure if they had even heard me. Connor hadn't shaved, so the shadow of a beard covered up part of his pale face.

His father had shaved, but I spotted two nicks on his chin. William's crow's-feet appeared deeper than usual. But it was Libby who seemed to have aged a decade over the past few days. Her skin was blotchy underneath her hair that hung in frizzy strands around her face. Libby's eyes were puffy, but she focused them on me.

"We're on our way out, but Momma wanted to ask you a favor." Connor reached over, kissed me on the cheek, and then whispered, "Please say yes. Momma is a mess."

My coffee churned in my stomach as I pulled away from Connor. Why would he think I'd say no to Libby? What in the world did she need me to do?

"What can I help you with, Libby?" I braced myself for her request.

"Could you go see Tessa around lunchtime today?" Libby rubbed her hands together in the cool morning air. "I need to be at the café with the cleaners all day, but I need to make sure Tessa is all right."

"You haven't seen her since that night? I grasped Libby's hands in the hope I would warm them as well as calm her nerves.

"No. I tried to get her to come over, but she said she was too upset." Libby sighed. "I understand, of course, but I'll feel better if someone sets eyes on her. Since I can't, I hoped that you would. She likes you."

"I'm happy to go see her. You said at lunchtime, so I assume you know that she'll be home then?" Libby's hands stopped trembling in my hands.

"Yes, she said had to go see Rob and Christine, but she'd be home by noon. Could you take lunch to her? She loves mac 'n' cheese from Frankie's. Let me give you money." Libby took her hands from mine and reached into her purse.

"No need, Libby. I've got this." I kissed her on the cheek. "Go to the café, and I'll call you after I see Tessa."

"You're such a doll. Connor, let's go." Libby smiled weakly. "After you say goodbye to your sweetheart, of course. Oh, Nubi, there you are, cutie pie."

Nubi sauntered out between my legs and rubbed up against Libby. She picked him up and buried her face in his fur. Nubi really did know when humans needed him.

"Thanks for helping, Momma," Connor said when his mother was out of earshot.

"I'm always happy to help her. Did you think I wouldn't?"

"That was my fault, Sammy." William came over and put his arm around me. "Libby has been out of her mind worrying about everything and everyone. I knew she would feel a little better if you were the one to see Tessa."

"Since Tessa likes me?"

"Yes, but your perspective on human nature and ability to solve puzzles will come in handy for this tragedy." William kissed the top of my head. "Thank you for helping. I'm off to speak with our landlord."

"Are you concerned about the café's lease?" I asked.

"Not really, but it doesn't hurt to check in with him. We've had a good relationship with him over the years and I don't see that changing. Libby isn't so sure, so I'm going to see him more for her than me."

William joined Libby and Nubi. He put his arm around her and pulled her close to his side. Nubi stretched his paw over to William, and the three of them looked like a happy family.

"My parents like being cat grandparents." Connor smiled.

"Nubi likes them, too." I put my hand on Connor's cheek. "How are you holding up? You've been your mother's rock throughout this."

"I'm happy I can help after everything she's done for me. I just wish she wasn't going through this. She loves her café." Connor held my hand and kissed it. "I'm sorry I haven't been around these past days—"

"Don't you even say that," I interrupted. "Your folks need you."

"They need you, too. And so do I." Connor smiled. "After all this, we need a romantic trip away."

"I'm going to hold you to that." I waved as Connor left with his parents. Nubi trotted back inside our apartment. I sat back down next to him and picked up my lukewarm coffee. The idea of a romantic getaway with Connor should have kept my mind busy, but all I could think about was solving this mystery. Visiting Tessa would be the next step in my plans.

11

Andrew insisted I take as long as I needed with Tessa.

"You must do anything you can to help Libby. I've never seen her so distraught." Andrew tapped a pen against his lips. "I can't describe her properly. She's just not herself."

Andrew was the best wordsmith I knew, so his concern for Libby must be overwhelming. I promised I would help Libby with Tessa, so at eleven thirty, I went to Frankie's Groceries to pick up lunch. Frankie made the best food, but she also served the best gossip.

"Hi, Frankie!" I entered the store and walked through the aisles. Not having a car wasn't a problem since I could find just about anything I needed or wanted here. From boxes of cereal to fresh fruit to toilet paper, the shop carried just about everything you could get from a larger grocery store. But the best part of Frankie's shop was her deli. Standing behind the counter in her white apron over a pumpkin-colored dress was Frankie Fortuna.

"Sammy! I'm so happy to see you." She wiped her hands

on her apron and lifted the hinged countertop to join me on the other side. "Frank said you came by last night, but I hoped you would come by again today."

"Why's that?" I asked after removing myself from Frankie's tight embrace.

"Now, you know I'm always happy to see you, but I wanted to know what's happening with that mess at Libby's." Frankie went back behind the counter. "Let me get Frank up here so he can take over while we talk."

Before I could tell Frankie I couldn't stay long, she had already opened the kitchen door and yelled for her grandson. Frank emerged from the kitchen with a tray of fried chicken.

"Hey, Sammy! Long time no see! How was last night's po boys?"

"They were fantastic. I'm glad I tried the catfish one for a change," I said. Frank was frying catfish when Sissy and I came into the shop last night. The aroma of the seasoned cornmeal-encrusted fish was too good to pass up.

"Well, now you can try my fried chicken." Frank grinned. The sparkle in his green eyes matched his grandmother's.

"*Your* fried chicken? That's a family recipe from decades ago." Frankie gave her grandson the evil eye.

"Fine, it's my version of the family recipe. I used homemade bacon salt on it. Come on, give it a try." Frank put the tray on the counter and pulled out a pair of tongs from a drawer. He grabbed two plates and put a drumstick on each one.

Frankie and I each took a plate. She sniffed the drumstick first, but I bit into it right away. I loved Frankie's fried chicken, but Frank's version was even better. The bacon salt added a touch of sweet and smoky flavor to the crisp batter on the chicken. Everyone had their favorite place for fried chicken from five-star restaurants to gas station convenience stores. Frankie's was mine even more so now.

"Frank, this is amazing." I grabbed a napkin to wipe my mouth after finishing my drumstick. "Sorry, Frankie, but your grandson's fried chicken is my new favorite."

"Don't tell anyone, but it's mine, too." Frankie grabbed the tongs and picked up another drumstick.

Frank grinned from ear to ear as he watched his grandmother eat another piece of chicken. Over the past few months, Frank was spending more time in the kitchen than making deliveries. His work was definitely paying off.

"Could I have two fried chicken meals, please? I'm taking lunch to a friend," I said.

"Yes, darling. Which friend? Everyone's got their favorite side dishes. If it's for Libby, she likes mac 'n' cheese and coleslaw." Frankie pulled out two take-out containers.

"Actually, it's for Tessa Ferguson. She works for Libby at the café."

"I know sweet Tessa. Poor thing must be beside herself." Frankie rested her head in her hands.

"I'm going to check on her. Libby's at the café with the cleaners, so I'm taking lunch to Tessa."

"And to find out what she knows about Griffin Black-thorn, too. I know you all too well, Sammy."

"Yes, you do, Frankie. And I know you well enough to know that you have some information for me."

"Guilty as charged!" Frankie's warm laugh was contagious, and I joined her.

"So, what do you have to tell me?"

"First, did you know Suzy was married? I didn't." Frankie frowned.

"No. Neither did Libby or Andrew. Did you know Suzy,

Tessa, Caleb, and Winston all came from Southern Pines?" I said.

As Frankie filled two take-out containers with fried chicken, mac 'n' cheese, and collard greens, she shared all that she knew about the group. The first time Caleb came into the store, he told Frankie that Suzy had recommended her gumbo. It was on his second visit that he asked if she was ready to retire and sell the building.

"Can you believe he asked me about retiring? Do I look like I can't run this place like I did when I was twenty? I've run this business, raised three children, and still have kept my girlish figure." Frankie did a spin, her apron strings flying as she twirled.

"He's apparently tried to buy or lease most of the buildings in the Quarter. Do you know where his office is? I haven't found it anywhere online," I said.

"I wonder if he actually has an office. If he does, I don't know." Frankie put the containers and a box of chocolate chip cookies into a grocery bag. "Ask that reporter Winston what's-his-name if he knows."

I laughed because Frankie knew Winston's last name. He shopped at her store, but he also came to her for information. But Frankie didn't like sharing with him. I'd like to say it's because she favored me over him. That might be part of it, but what Frankie understood, I wasn't looking for information to post on a blog. And my intentions were for the greater good. Winston, on the other hand...

"He calls himself a reporter, but he just stirs up trouble." Frankie sighed. "His flog, blog, whatever he calls it, always has negative things. I understand the world isn't perfect, but could he put something nice up for once?"

Frankie handed me the grocery bag. "I'll put this on your

tab, but the cookies are on me. Tell Tessa to come see me when she's feeling up to it."

"I will. Thanks for the food and everything else." I hugged Frankie and waved goodbye to Frank. The food smelled delicious so I headed straight toward Tessa's house. It wasn't only the food I was hungry for—I was hungry for information.

12

Tessa lived in a single shotgun cottage on Dumaine Street near Armstrong Park. Painted in vibrant orange and hunter green, the house stood out even among the typical brightly colored homes surrounding it. Leafy green plants in terra-cotta pots lined the steps. I knocked on the door, hoping Libby was right, that Tessa would be home.

A woman with short, spiky platinum hair, wearing a chef coat opened the door. "You have the wrong house. We didn't order food."

"Hi, I'm here for Tessa. My name is Sammy…"

"Tessa's not talking to the media." The woman started to shut the door.

"Wait, she's not a reporter." Tessa popped up behind the woman. "Sammy, what are you doing here?"

"Libby asked me to check on you. I brought lunch from Frankie's." I lifted the bag. "I'm sorry I didn't call ahead. Libby said you'd be home."

"Come inside." Tessa went into the living room and sat on a couch.

"Sorry if I seemed rude, but we've had people knocking ever since Griffin's death. I'm Lori, Tessa's roommate."

"I understand," I said.

"Tessa, I'm leaving for work. Call me if you need me." Lori picked up a bag by the door. She leaned close to me and whispered, "Thanks for coming over. She needs the company. Griffin was a jerk, but I couldn't convince her."

Lori closed the door behind her before I could ask her any more questions. I put the food bag on the coffee table and sat next to Tessa. Along with the couch, there were two side chairs and two beanbag chairs. The furniture was minimal, but the artwork was not.

A variety of framed photographs and paintings covered the walls. Rural landscapes, city streets, and flowers served as the subjects of both color and black-and-white photography. All the paintings, except for one, were floral watercolors. I didn't have to find the signature to recognize the painter of the canvas. Kudzu vines dropped over a white picket fence, continuing onto the cracked sidewalk.

"Griffin gave me that on the day he died." Tessa pushed herself off the sofa and stood by the painting. "It was a thank-you gift for setting up the show. I wish I'd never helped him. I wish I'd never met him."

Tessa took the painting down and faced it against the wall. She pulled her black cardigan sweater tightly around her body. Underneath, she wore jeans and a faded Jazz Fest T-shirt. She was barefoot, her pink toenails matching her hair. Both had seen better days as her polish was chipped, and her hair looked wild and unbrushed.

"Let me get drinks for us. Do you want a beer or a cocktail?"

"I'm working, so I'll pass on the drink. Y'all have quite the bar setup."

A glass cart in the far corner of the room displayed ten liquor bottles with different levels of liquid. Mismatched cocktail glasses filled the bottom shelf, including crystal highball glasses and champagne flutes, plastic Mardi Gras cups from various parades, and margarita glasses with cacti for stems. A dented silver ice bucket completed the bar.

"When I moved here, I learned you need lots of different liquors. Everyone makes fancy cocktails here, especially my roommate. But we have ice tea if you want that to drink."

"That would be great, thanks." While Tessa went to the kitchen, I took the food out of the bag and set it out on the coffee table. I moved a stack of books to the floor to make room. That's when I realized the book on the top was actually a photo album. I flipped it open and almost gasped.

Standing outside a café in a strip mall, the five people from Southern Pines smiled at the camera. A large, red ribbon blocked the doorway to The Pines Café. Griffin and Caleb stood on opposite sides of the door, each holding oversized scissors. Suzy had her hand on Griffin's shoulder as she stood next to her husband. Tessa and Winston were on Caleb's side, with Tessa closest to Caleb. Winston had his arm around her. A smile stretched across his face, and I noticed he didn't have the chip in his front tooth like he had now.

"That's when we all liked each other." Tessa put my ice tea in front of me. She sat down, took a gulp of her beer, and pointed at Griffin in the picture.

"Griffin and Caleb owned the café together. Caleb managed it, and Griffin brought in students as customers," she said.

"Really?" Funny how neither Griffin nor Caleb had mentioned that. "And as employees, by the looks of the T-shirts you and Winston were wearing."

"Winston and I were two of the first baristas."

"The café must have been a goldmine for material as a journalist."

Tessa let out a bitter laugh. "You've figured out what makes Winston tick. He's always called himself an investigative reporter. I used to find it attractive."

"When did that change?" I opened my box and took a bite of the creamy mac 'n' cheese.

Tessa put her beer down, settled back onto the sofa with her legs crisscrossed. "We dated our freshmen and sophomore years. He was smart, handsome, and ambitious. But during our junior year, he became ruthless."

I continued eating while Tessa shared Winston's transition from her happy boyfriend to her bitter ex-boyfriend. They spent less time together as Tessa took more art and photography classes. Winston's classes and position as editor of the school newspaper kept him busy. But Winston's relentless pursuit of being the first to break a story caused their relationship to crumble.

"Winston quit working at the café, but came in all the time. At first, I thought he was trying to spend time with me." Tessa finally took a bite of her food. "Then I realized he was there to spy on certain customers. When his big exposé on a grade for money scandal came out, I came to terms. I didn't matter as much as his story." Tessa didn't sound angry or sad. Her tone was matter of fact.

"I'm sorry."

"Don't be. It was the motivation I needed to break off the relationship."

"I think Winston didn't want to break up, considering how he kept trying to talk to you the other night," I said.

Tessa confirmed he didn't. He tried to win her back, especially when she spent more time with Griffin.

"Griffin was my thesis advisor. We met at the café a lot. Winston accused us of having an affair." Tessa turned beet red. "We weren't then, and we aren't now."

"I don't mean to be rude, but Suzy seemed to allude to the fact you were," I said gently, hoping I wouldn't offend her.

"I know, but we've always been friends. But the past few months, Griffin said he and Suzy were discussing a divorce." Tessa's eyes watered. "I won't deny that I hoped if he was single we could..."

Tessa sobbed and buried her head in her hands. I put my arm around her as she cried. After a minute, she raised her head and grabbed a napkin to wipe her tears.

"You must be going through so many emotions, Tessa." I handed her another napkin.

"I am! I'm sad Griffin is dead, but I'm angry he used me. All he wanted was the show at Libby's."

"And he wanted Caleb to get Libby's café for him." For a second, it felt wrong to make her feel bad about Libby, but I needed to know if she was aware of that plan.

"I had no idea he wanted Libby's café. You have to believe me." Tessa grasped my hand so hard that I flinched. "Libby is the kindest boss I've ever had. I'd never want to hurt her."

I slowly pulled my hand away. "Libby knows that. She's worried about you. You should call her."

"I want to, but I'm embarrassed. First, she must think I'm an idiot for believing Griffin was divorcing Suzy. Second, I had no idea he wanted her place." Tessa gulped the rest of her beer. "And finally, he dies after drinking her coffee."

I opened the box of cookies and ate one. I needed a moment to decide how to respond. Libby brought the coffee to the table, but Tessa made it. She appeared distraught over

Griffin's death; many murderers felt remorseful after the fact. Reminding her she made the drinks might end our conversation, so I didn't.

"The police are working hard to figure out what happened, so that everyone, including you and Libby, will be cleared," I said.

"Thanks. I really hope so for Libby. Maybe I'm just bad luck. The Pines Café closed just before I graduated."

"What happened?"

"Caleb managed the café, but he started doing more real estate deals. He let things go, at least according to Griffin. I came to work one day, and the doors were padlocked." Tessa's cell phone rang. "It's Lori. I need to talk to her." She answered the call. "Hi. I'm okay. Yes, Sammy's still here but she's leaving soon."

I took the hint and gathered my trash. "I need to get back to work. Let me and Libby know if you need anything."

"Just leave your trash. The least I can do is clean up." Tessa followed me to the front door. "Thanks for lunch."

Tessa opened the door and scanned the area. Was she looking for reporters or someone she knew, like Winston or Caleb? The sidewalk was empty. Tessa gave me a quick hug and returned to her call as she shut the door. I was glad she had a roommate who was looking out for her. She seemed upset, but she could be a good liar. I couldn't take her off the suspect list yet. But she gave me new information. Now I just needed to confirm it and decide if the past in Southern Pines had anything to do with the present.

13

Walking back to the shop, I had to take a detour. I couldn't miss a chance to talk to Caleb, especially after what Tessa told me. He stood at the end of the block in front of a vacant storefront. The glass in the windows and door were covered in plywood, with a real estate sign hanging where the café's sign used to be. Caleb tried opening the door with the handle, but what he did next surprised me even more. He took a leather case out of his front pocket and unzipped it. He took out a small metal tool and put it in the lock. Caleb was trying to pick the lock. Wow, that was either brave or stupid to be doing that in the daylight. From his frantic gestures, it appeared his lock-pick wasn't working. He shoved the pick back in the set and into his pocket.

I wanted to catch him before he left, so I raced quickly halfway down the block. I slowed down for the last half of the block so it would appear that I just happened upon him.

"Hey, Caleb." I casually walked up to him.

"Samantha, hello." He shoved his hands in his pockets

and looked at me like a child caught with his hand in the cookie jar.

"Hi. How are you? Great day for a walk, isn't it?" I decided not to confront him about trying to break into the café. Accusing him of breaking and entering wouldn't get me any answers afterward.

"Good, good. Yes, a great day to stroll around the neighborhood." The tension in his face disappeared. "Do you know anything about this building?"

"It was a lovely café with the most amazing coffee cake. A kitchen fire destroyed the entire place a month ago. Didn't you hear about it?"

"No. I guess I missed it. So the whole place is gutted? That's a shame." Caleb sighed.

I bit my tongue and didn't say, *You sound like it's a shame for you, not the owners.* Instead, I said, "Are you still looking for a café? Do you have other clients besides Griffin who want a one?"

"Do you know of any for sale?" Caleb took his phone out and stared at a map.

"Not off hand, but I'll let you know," I lied.

"Thanks. I'm anxious to find a place and get settled."

"Are you looking to open a café yourself? I heard you and Griffin owned one in Southern Pines."

"Who told you that?" Caleb looked up from his phone.

"Tessa did. She said she and Winston worked there."

"We did own a café together. After I got into real estate, and Griffin put more time into his teaching career, we closed it." Caleb went back to his map.

"If you don't mind me saying, I'm surprised you would want to open another café since you're into real estate here. You and Griffin must have had a great working relationship besides your friendship," I said.

Caleb didn't say a word, but closed the map app. He stared at me, I assumed to make me feel uncomfortable at asking a pointed question. It didn't work; I held his gaze. He broke first.

"I'm confident I can run a café, along with my real estate business. And yes, Griffin and I were good friends and future business partners again," he said.

"Sorry, I didn't mean to offend you." I smiled and Caleb relaxed his face. "It's just that I know how hard it is to run a business, and I have an amazing partner in Andrew. Now that Griffin is gone, I can only imagine how much work will land on your shoulders. Good for you for wanting to continue with the plans you and Griffin made."

"It'll be tough, but I'll do it in Griffin's memory." Caleb sighed. "So you don't know of any places for sale?"

I wanted to keep talking with Caleb, so I lied. "You know, I think there was a sign on a property near Rampart Street. I'll recognize it when I see it. Come on, I'll show you."

Caleb opened his mouth probably to protest he didn't need me, but he didn't. He snapped his mouth shut and smiled widely. "I'd appreciate that. If you have the time."

"It won't take long to get there." I started toward Rampart Street, and Caleb walked next to me.

"Now this part of the Quarter is mostly residential with a few bars and restaurants. Did you know Marie Laveau lived on St. Ann? My friend owns her house. Well, not exactly her house since the original was torn down by mistake."

"By mistake? Did Marie sue?"

"Do you know who Marie Laveau is, or rather, was?"

Caleb shook his head, so I gave him a brief synopsis of the history of Marie Laveau, New Orleans's Voodoo Queen. He laughed when I told him she died in 1881 and the house was torn down in 1903.

"I'm out of touch with New Orleans history. Past and present, I guess," Caleb said.

"Well, if you're going to live and work here, I'd suggest taking a few tours. You'll learn a lot about the city and the neighborhood."

"I'll keep that in mind." Caleb stopped walking and turned to me. "You're being awfully friendly, considering your friend Libby was pretty mad the night Griffin died."

"Well, if I help you find a place, you won't bother trying to get Libby's lease out from under her," I lied. After William talked to their landlord, he assured them he wasn't interested in leasing the café to anyone else but Libby. But being nice to Caleb now would hopefully get me more information about his relationship with Griffin and the others.

"You really care about her, don't you?" Caleb said.

"Yes, I do. She treated me as a friend the first time I met her in the café. And then she rented an apartment to me. My life here started with Libby's kindness," I said.

"Sounds nice." Caleb's tone wasn't sarcastic but wistful. For a moment I felt bad for him, but then I remembered he was a murder suspect.

"Hey, Sammy! Wait up!" Beau Boudreaux called from across the street. Dressed in jeans and an aqua cashmere sweater, his smile was as bright as his glossy black hair.

"Hi, Beau!" I hugged him after he joined Caleb and me. "Do you know Caleb Rhodes?"

"Yes, we met briefly at a chamber of commerce party." Beau offered his hand to Caleb. "You haven't been back to a meeting, though."

"You have a great memory." Caleb shook Beau's hand. "I'm afraid I became so busy working, so I haven't made it back."

"I understand. You're a real estate agent, right?" Beau asked.

"Caleb is also looking to open a coffee shop, too, " I said. "You should talk to Beau. He's owned a lot of businesses here, including a bar."

"Really?" Caleb's demeanor perked up. "Do you still own businesses? Or are you looking to sell or lease any properties?"

"Not at this time, but we can talk further. Are you looking to buy real estate just for your clients, or is the coffee shop just for you?" Beau said.

"I like selling real estate, but I'm opening a café here, too," Caleb said.

I stepped back and pretended to answer a phone call. Caleb seemed relaxed around Beau as a fellow business owner, so I hoped he'd chat more in depth with him.

"I'll be honest. The restaurant industry is tough, especially here. Do you have a business partner, or is this as a sole proprietor?" Beau asked.

"I did have a partner, but he died recently," Caleb said.

"I'm sorry to hear that. Are you looking for another partner? If it was a fifty-fifty business, losing half the investment would be tough," Beau said sympathetically. "Once you've got your finances settled, give me a call. I'd be happy to introduce you to my friends in the restaurant community."

"That would be fantastic." Caleb grinned. "Actually, my finances are fine. Well, they will be soon. My partner and I had insurance policies on each other. I never thought we'd need them."

"Better safe than sorry, I say. You and your business partner did the right thing." Beau handed his business card to Caleb. "Here's my number. Call me next week and we can talk."

"I will. Thank you." Caleb put the card in a scuffed brown wallet. "I need to run to a meeting, but I'm glad we met again today."

"You can thank Sammy for our reintroduction. I'll always say hello to my favorite redhead." Beau winked at me.

"Yes, thanks, Sammy." Caleb smiled, but I wondered if it was just for Beau's benefit. He offered more to Caleb than I did. "I'll look for that property on Rampart another time. See you both later."

I waved as I pretended to end my phone conversation. Caleb power-walked down the street. Once he was out of earshot, Beau said, "How did I do? Did I get some information for you that you needed for your investigation? He had a motive to kill Griffin. I wonder how much insurance he had on him."

"My investigation? I think it's yours after that chat." I laughed. "You did great. Did Andrew tell you about him?"

"He did last night. It took two Vieux Carres to tell the whole story."

Beau and Andrew loved drinking their favorite cocktail at the Carousel Bar at Hotel Monteleone. Only in New Orleans would there be a bar designed like a carousel, but with barstools instead of carved animals to ride. The seats didn't go up and down, but the bar did rotate slowly. I occasionally joined them, but stuck to my favorite cocktail, the Pimm's Cup.

"How many turns did the carousel take while y'all talked?"

"I never count. But really, was I helpful?"

"Definitely. I'd take you for a drink, but I need to get back to the shop."

"Yep, that coworker of yours is a taskmaster." He

laughed. "Don't tell him I said that. Actually, that's what he says about you."

"You're such a liar. We love working together, even more than your beloved Vieux Carres."

Beau gasped, placing a hand on his chest. "Do not mock the best cocktail in the world, young lady."

"Noted, young man." I went up on my tiptoes and kissed him on the cheek. "Drinks are on me next time."

"I'll hold you to it. See you later, darling." Beau headed in the opposite direction I needed to go, so I hurried to the shop on my own. I needed the time to myself to go over the new information I learned. But it also brought up more questions—who else had insurance on Griffin? And if Suzy was the intended victim, who had insurance on her?

14

———————

I had returned to work after meeting with Tessa and Caleb. Beau had already called Andrew, so he knew about their conversation. But I told him about Caleb's lock-picking attempt.

"My, that is interesting," Andrew had said. "He's up further on the suspect list now, isn't he? You already know he has criminal tendencies."

Andrew also agreed that Tessa couldn't be excluded from the suspect list. He offered to ask his fellow professors at Tulane if they were familiar with Griffin's time at the university. "Someone should know something about him, especially if he was rumored to have an inappropriate student-teacher relationship," Andrew had said.

I called Libby and left her a message when her phone went directly to voicemail. Hopefully that meant she was busy with the cleaners and not fretting over the state of her business. My report on Tessa would hopefully make her feel better.

I spent the afternoon dealing with spreadsheets, invoices, and correspondence, so I didn't have a moment to contemplate on who was Griffin's killer. Well, I was calling it murder, but the police were still officially calling it a "suspicious death." Sissy texted me when I was walking home to tell me and that she had no new information from Rob. A frowning emoji ended her text. She really needed an emoji of her own for when Rob wouldn't tell her anything.

Connor waited for me inside my apartment with a pan of shepherd's pie and a pecan pie that Libby had made for us. Over a delicious meal, we talked about our day. Connor made his way to his parents' place to keep his mom company after spending a few hours playing on Royal Street. She was thrilled with the work the professional cleaners did, but she was also nervous about reopening the café. To keep her mind off her worries, she cooked when she returned to her apartment.

"I wish your mom and dad would have joined us. You'll have to take the rest of the pie up to them," I said in between bites of pecan pie. I savored the soft, sweet filling and the buttery crunchy pecans on top. A dollop of homemade whipped cream added the perfect lightness to the piece of pie.

"Momma said not to bring any of it home. The kitchen is full of pies, cookies, and cakes," Connor said.

"She needs to get back into the café and bake." I stole a bit of Connor's whipped cream.

"Hey, that's mine. There's more in the fridge." Connor playfully elbowed me. "Momma is going into the café tomorrow to get ready to reopen. We should enjoy her home cooking while we can."

After we finished the pie, there was a knock at the door.

"Come on in!" I called as the door swung open.

"You're really too relaxed about welcoming people into your home, Sammy." Neal Bennett ruffled my hair as he beelined to the pecan pie on the counter. No matter when my upstairs neighbor came by, he always headed for any food I had out. His trim, athletic physique must be the result of all the walking he did as the owner of a tour guide company. "We could have been a killer, a burglar, or worse —Ruby."

"Come on, Ruby isn't so bad. She means well in her own way." Jasper St. Martin picked up Nubi from one of my chairs. He sat down, and Nubi left his hair on Jasper's Past & Present Tours T-shirt before curling up in his lap. Nubi always went to Jasper when he came to visit. Somehow, he knew Jasper was my cousin, so they were family. But Nubi could also sense when someone needed comforting, and Jasper was still mourning the loss of his girlfriend.

"Just like your momma." Connor went to the kitchen and moved Neal away from the pie. "Aunt Charlene sent me an article about musicians needing at least two other jobs to be financially stable."

"I'd apologize for her, but thankfully you understand her," Jasper said.

"No worries. I like your momma." Connor sliced two pieces of pie and put a healthy serving of whipped cream on both. He handed one to Neal and took the other to Jasper, along with a small dish of whipped cream for Nubi.

"Speaking of moms, how's yours, Connor?" Neal sat cross-legged on the floor by the coffee table.

"Momma is stressed, to say the least, but she's getting through it. She told me to tell you thanks for the flowers." Connor sat next to me.

"It was Jasper's idea, but I'll take part of the credit for remembering Libby likes pink roses." Neal used his fork to scrape the last of the whipped cream off his plate. "Connor, you were stingy with the pie and whipped cream."

"You think half a pie is a serving." Connor laughed. "I'm saving the rest for Sissy and Rob. They're both working."

"Are you trying to bribe Rob with pie to get information?" Neal grinned.

"If only that would work." I sighed.

"You're investigating on your own, aren't you?" Jasper rubbed his crescent-moon scar, which he only did when he was worried or stressed. "Please be careful."

I reached across the table and squeezed Jasper's hand. While I appreciated all the love from my friends, whom I considered family, Jasper and his mom were my only blood relatives, and I had a special spot in my heart for them.

"I promise I'm being careful. Now, tell me what's going on with Aunt Charlene. She left me a rambling message about Annabeth leaving Huntley."

With the deaths of her husband and daughter and then Jasper moving to New Orleans, Aunt Charlene was left on her own. Her friend Annabeth moved in with her and they began traveling together, especially cruises. From the video calls she made from the ships, they both were having a great time, meeting new people and seeing the world.

"She decided to move to Montana to live with a guy she met on their last Caribbean cruise. Momma is happy for her, but thinks she's crazy for moving to 'that cold as a leftover turducken in the back of a freezer state.'" Jasper replicated his mother's deep drawl.

All four of us laughed, but then Jasper's face grew serious. "I'm worried about Momma being alone now. She really loved living with Annabeth, more than living with my dad, I think. She's never lived alone."

"You're not moving back in with her, are you?" I tried to speak calmly, but it came out high-pitched.

"No! New Orleans is my home now." Jasper jumped up, came around the table, and hugged me.

I hugged him closely. Ever since his girlfriend was murdered, I worried Jasper would leave. Fortunately, he embedded himself even more into the community by joining a Mardi Gras krewe and applying for college in the spring. Living in New Orleans gave Jasper the life he hoped for, but I couldn't deny I wanted him to stay here for me, too. Jasper sat back down, and Neal patted him on the back.

"I told Jasper Aunt Charlene can move to New Orleans, but we don't have room in our apartment. Maybe you'd like to share your place with her, Sammy?" Neal said.

"No," Connor and I said in unison.

"Listen, I love Aunt Charlene, but we're not roommate material." I grinned. "We'll talk to her at Thanksgiving and figure out what she wants to do."

"She's coming for Thanksgiving, but she's also staying for your birthday. Did she tell you?" Jasper said.

"Which birthday? You have two of them, don't you?" Neal said.

Neal was right. There was the actual day I was born and the day my adopted parents decided was my birthday. They were only a few days off my actual birthday. But I had only learned the date when Aunt Charlene and Jasper came into my life. I hadn't given the actual date much thought. Legally, I abided by the date my parents picked.

"Yes, I hadn't planned on celebrating both. For thirty years, I've celebrated November 25."

"You mean twenty-eight years," Jasper said.

Connor put his arm around me as I took in a deep breath. Jasper was correct since I had been lost to my birth family when I was two during a hurricane. This was drumming up more emotions than I wanted to deal with tonight.

"You're right. But don't worry, y'all only have to get me one gift, not two." I laughed, trying to shake off an impending feeling of sadness. I should think of the bright side of having two birthdays: two birthday cakes. But I couldn't help but worry that on my actual birthday all I would think about was the life, and more importantly, the family, I lost.

15

———————

A cold snap arrived making it a restless night for me and Nubi. I woke up around 3:00 a.m. to find Nubi wrapped around my head, trying to steal my body heat. Turning up the thermostat helped the chill in the air, but it didn't help me get back to sleep. I kept replaying the evening of Griffin's murder, trying to remember some detail that would help. Finally I gave up about an hour later when Nubi meowed and curled up next to me. Nubi looked after me better than I did myself.

The morning's sun warmed my face as I walked to Lagniappe Books. The plethora of "good mornings" warmed my heart, though. I loved living in a place where acknowledging your neighbors or even strangers was normal and actually expected. When I lived in San Francisco, no one made eye contact, let alone say hi when walking past each other on the street or even if you lived in the same apartment building.

Today was my day off, but I wanted to unpack a large delivery that came in yesterday. Andrew insisted he could handle it. He ran the shop without me for many years, so he truly didn't need my help. But restocking books was his least favorite thing to do, and I didn't mind. While we didn't track our time in the shop, I didn't want my investigating to affect my professional life.

But this morning, investigating would come before work. Suzy stood outside her shop with Rob and Christine. I was torn between casually walking over or leaving them alone. Fortunately, I didn't have to decide.

"Sammy! Darling, come over here! You can back up what I'm saying." Suzy waved frantically.

I crossed the street and joined them. "Good morning, y'all. Is there any news?"

"If you mean have they figured Griffin's death out, no, there is no news." Suzy glared at Rob and Christine who didn't react. I wondered if they practiced those blank stares in the mirror together.

"We understand Suzy and Griffin switched coffee mugs. We just had more questions about it." Rob's tone wasn't accusatory, but Suzy didn't see it that way.

"I told you he took my mug that night," Suzy insisted.

"Actually, ma'am, it was Sammy who told us." Christine paged through her notebook. "She said Griffin claimed you had his drink, the almond milk latte."

"Oh. Well, I must have been too upset to say anything." Suzy frowned. "But yes, he said my cup smelled like the almond milk. But I didn't notice a difference."

"Was this a habit of his, to check your coffee if his didn't seem right?" Rob asked.

"Um, no, actually I don't think he ever did." Suzy's eyes filled with tears. "If he didn't think it was almond milk, he'd go back to the barista and make them redo it. Do you think if he had, he'd be alive?"

"We're still investigating, Miss Suzy, but we'll get back to you as soon as we can," Rob said.

"One more question before we go." Christine flipped open her notebook and reached a page. "You have a million-dollar life insurance policy on your husband. We noticed there were two policies on you totaling two million dollars. Is there a reason for this?"

"Two million dollars? Are you sure? Griffin and I applied for life insurance together when we got married, but it was for a million each." Suzy's eyes were dry now, and her mouth twisted in a grimace.

"Yes, ma'am. The second million-dollar policy was taken out a year ago. You don't recall this?" Christine asked.

"I would remember this. I need to call the insurance company now. Excuse me." Suzy took her keys out of her purse and opened the door. "You'll let me know if you discover anything else, won't you?"

Before Rob or Christine could answer, Suzy shut the door and locked it behind her.

"I'd say it's looking more and more like Suzy was the intended victim. Is that what y'all are thinking?" I asked.

"Sammy, you know we're not going to answer." Christine put her notebook in her jacket pocket.

"But we do have a question for you about the sugar packets. Libby said she only carries the 'fake sugar,' as she calls it, from the company who uses yellow packets. And we understand you were the one to refill the tabletop holders for them. Did you happen to put any pink ones in?"

"I've never seen the pink ones at Libby's." I shook my head. "Hold it. There were a few pink packets under the table, weren't there? That seems an easy way to bring in poison. Did you test those? How about the coffee mugs and spilled coffee?"

Rob and Christine looked at each other but didn't say a word. I kept pushing.

"It was poison, right? Cyanide?"

"Yes, it was cyanide," Rob answered. "It's going to be public knowledge tonight."

"Where was it found? Besides in Griffin, of course." I shuddered, thinking of the poison taking over his body.

"That is still to be determined. Christine, there's no harm in saying that. Tests are ongoing is what the chief will say later."

Christine had coughed loudly while Rob spoke, then said, "Yes, he will. But let's not encourage Sammy. Remember, she's not a detective."

"But we do appreciate your information. Is there anything you'd like to share?" Rob raised his eyebrows at me.

"No. I imagine you've already learned about everyone's past in Southern Pines. That's all I've heard."

"Contact us if you do learn anything. Thanks, Sammy." Rob patted my shoulder as he took out his phone and headed a few feet away from me.

"If you remember anything else, call us. Don't get into any trouble, okay?" Christine gave me her trademark stare, which made you feel guilty even if you didn't do anything.

"I promise I'll let y'all know if I remember anything."

Christine joined Rob, and they left me alone in front of Suzy's store wondering if they'd found cyanide in the sugar packets. If so, someone went to a lot of trouble to bring in the poison. But who was the real target? Suzy or Griffin?

16

———

I quickly unpacked the boxes at the shop, left a note for Andrew to call me if anything else came in today, and then raced to Artistic Coffee and Creations.

"Come on in, Sammy. You're just in time to help with the cleansing." Libby opened the door and ushered me.

"Cleaning or cleansing?" I asked.

"The cleansing, of course!" Libby said.

Even if I hadn't known that the café had been professionally cleaned yesterday, I knew that Libby was referring to a spiritual cleaning. Ruby and Papa weren't there to mop the floors. Ruby, the spiritualist and psychic, wore even more scarves than normal over her floor-length, white silk dress. She waved her ring-laden hands in the air as if she were batting away mosquitos. Papa, a Voodoo priest, was also dressed in white, wearing pants and a long-sleeve button-up shirt. The overhead lights shined down on his bald head and his tarnished brass python-topped cane. He always carried it, but I'd noticed lately it was more for show than functionality. Spending more time with Ruby seemed to have helped his limp and put a smile on his face more often.

"I'm glad to help, Libby. Where are Griffin's paintings?" I said.

The café's walls were bare. Griffin's work had vanished.

"Suzy took them yesterday. Honestly, I was glad she did. I didn't want people coming in just to see his work," Libby said. "But I didn't ask her to do it. Caleb came with her."

"Caleb?"

"I was surprised, too." Libby shrugged her shoulders. "Apparently, he's been helping her with the financial aspects of Griffin's affairs. Poor Suzy cried as they wrapped up the paintings."

"What do you mean by financial aspects?" My stomach dropped at the thought of Caleb telling Suzy to sue Libby.

"From what I gathered, he was helping her with Griffin's life insurance policy and recommended she auction off his paintings. I overheard him say that the paintings are worth more now that he's dead." Libby shook her head slowly.

"That's a pretty tacky thing to say just a few days after Griffin died," I said.

"Oh, I agree, and so did Suzy. At least she told him that was a horrible thing to say. But then I noticed her studying the paintings more seriously after that," Libby said. "Do you think she needs money? Her store is always busy."

"I don't know about her finances, but I agree that her store appears successful," I said. "Was Caleb right about the value of the paintings? I'm sure there's a market for artwork by murder victims." I shivered at the thought that Griffin's work would be popular because he had been killed. But what disturbed me even more was the possibility that auctioning the paintings could have been the reason for his death.

"The value might go up, but there's no guarantee," Libby said.

"Come on over here so we can begin. I do not have all day," Ruby said.

Libby pulled me over to the table where Griffin had died. Ruby and Papa stood around the table, each fiddling with their own tools of their trades. Ruby had four bundles of sage, a box of matches, and a heart-shaped white crystal. Papa had a jar of red powder and a ball of twigs floating in water inside a coffee cup.

"What did you bring, Papa?" I asked.

"The jar is redbrick dust. I'll put a line of it outside the front door to keep evil out," he said. "Now don't worry, Libby, it'll just be a small line, so the folks won't track it in."

"Oh, I don't mind cleaning up brick dust if it keeps the evil out." Libby rubbed her hands together.

"What's in the mug?" I asked.

"This is the Rose of Jericho. It will ward off evil spirits and negative energy. It looks like a ball of twigs, but in about four hours it will turn green. Libby, you will need to keep it in this mug for seven days to receive its full effects."

"I recognized it as the resurrection plant in Catholicism. My granny put one out every Easter when I was a child," Libby said.

"It's so interesting how the same things are used in so many religions," I said.

"And in personal spiritual practices." The tone Ruby used reminded me of my math teacher correcting me for the fifth time during a calculus class.

"Very true." Papa smiled at Ruby. "Now, Ruby, would you like to explain what you have planned?"

"Ruby, I recognize your favorite herb, sage. Wouldn't

mint be better in a café?" I reached for the sage, but Ruby picked up all the bundles first.

Ruby ignored my comment. "Libby, we will need to open the windows to allow the smoke and the negative energy to leave. We can wait to open the front door at the end of our smudging."

I helped Libby open the windows. The circles under her eyes had disappeared, and her movements were purposeful. Whether she believed in Ruby and Papa's rituals, it seemed to have given her a renewed sense of hope.

Ruby lit the bundles of sage and handed one to each of us. "Twenty seconds after I light these bundles, we will blow out the sage and we will walk through the café. Libby will go behind the counter and into the kitchen. Samantha will take the restrooms and the area in front of the counter. Papa and I will cleanse the main room."

"What do we do after that?" Libby asked.

"Come to the front door when you're done. We will gather there and open the door together and let out the negativity." Ruby looked directly at me, and as tempted as I was to make a snarky remark, I didn't. This meant too much to Libby, and I would do anything to help her.

We did as Ruby instructed, and I had to admit I felt the energy shift in the room. When I walked into the café, it felt cold and sterile with the empty bakery case and tables and the lack of artwork. The room felt heavy. Even though the room remained empty, a sense of lightness filled the café. Ruby would argue it was the sage, though it might actually be the sunlight streaming through the windows. Maybe it was the sage, but Libby's joyful expression convinced me that her attitude shaped the atmosphere.

"My Goddess of Good, I call upon you to aid us in removing the negative energy. Help bring in the love and light for dear Libby as she reopens her beloved café for the community." Ruby then opened the door. "Everyone come here. Papa, bring your brick dust, please."

We did as instructed. Papa spread a thin line of brick dust along the threshold.

"Any spirits who wish harm or disruption must leave now. Be gone!" Ruby slammed the door with such force that it rattled the doorframe. "We are done. The café is now cleansed, Libby, so you can proceed safely."

"Thank you, Ruby! And Papa!" Libby pulled the two of them into a hug. "I feel so much better."

"You're welcome." Ruby pulled away from the embrace first, but I caught her smiling for a second.

"Ruby, is Griffin's ghost here?" I figured it didn't hurt to ask. I'd take any clues from anyone, including the deceased victim.

"No, he is not. Griffin's spirit must have crossed over," Ruby answered. "Now, Libby, you'll have to excuse me. I have an appointment at my shop in twenty minutes."

"I need to go, too. But remember to keep the Rose of Jericho in a safe place for seven days." Papa joined Ruby at the table and gathered their materials.

As Libby took the mug with the plant behind the bakery counter, I said to Papa and Ruby, "Y'all have made Libby feel so much better. It was very kind of you to help her."

"We always help our friends and family." Papa hugged me. "How are you, my dear? Are you carrying your gris-gris bag?"

Papa made me a gris-gris bag every few weeks. I'd never had one before moving to New Orleans; I didn't really know much about Voodoo either. Any time I went by his store, Papa's Spirits & Charms, he would either "refresh" my leather pouch with more eucalyptus oil or create a new one from scratch. Gris-gris charms were usually made from sachets and held a particular combination of herbs, oils, and stones. The materials used depended on what the owner of it needed—love, money, luck, and, in my case, protection.

I patted my left hand jeans pocket. "Yes, it's in here. And Ruby's crystal is in my pocket, too."

Ruby gave a quick smile, but I caught it. She had given me an obsidian stone months ago, and I kept it on me most days. The shiny black oval stone would protect me from emotional or physical harm. Again, I wasn't sure if either item protected me, but it couldn't hurt. And knowing there were people out there who cared enough to share their beliefs with me made me feel good. I opened the front door for them and waited as they walked down the street. While they denied they were romantically involved, I had my doubts. Their genuine smiles and affectionate touches with each other seemed to say they were more than friends.

It wasn't my business, of course, but Papa was one of my favorite people, and I was glad to see him happy. He had been a widower since Hurricane Katrina, and his relationship with Ruby over the past few months appeared to be his first since then.

I had no idea of Ruby's former romantic relationships. Even her daughter, Verity, knew nothing about Ruby's love life, including who her father was. That was one mystery I wouldn't try to solve unless Verity asked me, and even then I'd have to consider the wrath of Ruby.

Right now, the only mystery I needed to solve was who killed Griffin.

17

———

Just as I started to shut the door, a voice yelled from down the street, "Sammy! Don't shut the door just yet!"

Rushing toward the café door was Terry Faucheaux and his friend Jimmy following close behind. I did a double take, as I rarely saw them outside The Gas Light. Usually they sat at their regular table playing poker using the stale peanuts from the community bowl. Today they were pushing a large industrial laundry cart. Once they reached the door I saw the cart was filled with paintings.

"Cher, keep the door open while these two old men push this on through," Terry said.

"Speak for yourself, old man. I'm younger than you." Jimmy grinned.

"If that's the case, then push this on through yourself, young'un." Terry entered the café, leaving Jimmy on the sidewalk behind the cart. "Sammy, what are you doing here?"

"I'm here helping Libby get ready for tomorrow's opening. What are you doing with all these paintings?"

"Libby needed artwork, so Terry brought his. It's about time he showed them to everyone." Jimmy pushed the cart through the door.

"Your artwork, Terry?" I had always assumed Terry was a house painter not a fine-arts painter. His pants and hands always had traces of paint, but he never mentioned artwork. Nor had he mentioned house painter so that was wrong of me to assume that was his job.

"Yes, it's mine. It's a hobby really, but Libby thinks they're good enough to go on the walls here." Terry blushed for the first time in front of me.

Libby came out of the kitchen and squealed. "Terry, you brought your work! I'm so happy you did."

"Anything for you, cher." He hugged Libby after she rushed over. "Now, you just pick what you like. If you don't like anything, you won't hurt my feelings."

"I've been begging you for years to show your art here. Everyone is going to love it." Libby began pulling artwork out of the basket with Jimmy's help.

"Here, let me help Jimmy." I took Libby's spot so she and Terry could place them against the walls. Once the paintings were all out, Terry and Libby discussed where they should go.

"I want this one over in the center of the two windows." Libby picked up a painting I hadn't seen. "You and Connor should be center stage, Sammy."

"Terry, you painted me and Connor?" I rushed over to Libby and stared at the painting of Connor and me on the corner of Royal and St. Peters. In front of the grocery store, Connor played his trumpet while I stood on the side smiling at him. The painting almost looked like a photograph with the attention to detail—from Connor's fingers on the trumpet keys to the Open sign on Rouse's door. Terry captured the joy of the music scene on the street and that of Connor and me.

"I almost held this one back, but Libby insisted I bring it." Terry took the canvas from Libby and hung it on the nail left by Griffin's painting. "It was going to be a wedding gift, but y'all are taking your good ole time with that."

"Terry, we haven't even been dating a year!" I laughed. "But you'll be one of the first to know if we get engaged."

"You mean *when* not *if*." Libby kissed me on the cheek.

"No pressure, Sammy." Jimmy joined us and winked at me.

"Let's get back to the paintings. Who else have you painted?" I wanted to change the subject. Connor and I were happy with our relationship as it was, so I didn't want to talk about weddings. This was the best relationship I'd been in, and I didn't want to jinx it with engagement talk.

Terry's paintings were all magnificent. I recognized many of the people on the canvas: Neal guiding a group into St. Louis Cathedral, Sissy and Rob sitting at the Café Beignet patio, and Rose behind the bar at The Gas Light. He captured the French Quarter perfectly in each work. From the expressions of the people on the street to the architectural details in each building, his talent was obvious.

Libby and Terry put up the description cards for each painting as they hung them where Griffin's paintings had been. Jimmy and I waited by the laundry basket as they finished.

"So, Jimmy, is painting Terry's full-time profession?"

Jimmy laughed. "You thought he was a house painter, didn't you?"

My face grew warm. "I'm embarrassed to say yes, but it's true."

"Darling, don't be embarrassed. Terry doesn't tell people

he's a painter. He has been known to paint a house if a friend needs it done, so he lets people believe that's what he does." Jimmy shook his head. "He's so good at it, but in his family you either own a mechanic shop or wrestle gators. No one is an artist."

"Come on, you're making that up." I grinned.

"No, I'm serious." Jimmy kept a straight face. "His grandpappy and daddy owned auto repair shops. Is that hard to believe?"

"You smart aleck." I put my hands on my hips. "I'd believe the wrestling-gator vocation for him, though. But really, what does Terry do for a living?"

Jimmy bent down and whispered in my ear, "Don't tell him I told you. Terry owns The Gas Light."

"What?" If I was a cartoon character, my eyes would have popped out of my face. "You're kidding, right?"

"Nope. He's owned it for forty years. Terry got it in his second divorce settlement. The ex got the gator farm. Now, you've got to promise not to tell him you know about this. He'll tell you when he's ready."

I stared at Jimmy, trying to decide if he was serious. He was smiling but not with the *I got you* smile but the sincere smile. I was more inclined to believe him than not. Terry always seemed to be at the bar, and anyone else who owned the place would have gotten rid of the bowls of stale peanuts a long time ago. Only an owner would keep them to use for poker games.

Before I could question Jimmy more, Libby and Terry joined us. As much as I wanted to ask Terry about the bar, I didn't. I'd learned it was better to respect the person who asks you to keep information to yourself. If you don't, you won't get any more in the future.

Confirming Terry's ownership of The Gas Light really wasn't necessary. I was just curious. The information I really needed today was about Griffin and my suspects for his murder. Terry's past would just have to wait for the day he was ready to tell me...if ever.

18

Even if I wanted to follow Terry out of the café and to The Gas Light, I had too much to do. Libby's employees arrived just as Terry and Jimmy left. Even though it had only been a few days since the café closed, they greeted each other like it was a family reunion. Everyone jumped in to reset the tables, refill the espresso machine and coffee makers, and to set the kitchen back up for baking. The only person missing was Tessa.

"I asked her to come, but she said it was too soon," Libby explained when I asked her about her missing employee. "Do you think she'll ever come back?"

"She's still hurting, but I know she cares about you. Give her some time." For Libby's sake, I hoped Tessa would return to the café. If she came back, my guess was Libby would feel better that Griffin's death hadn't ruined their relationship. For me, it would mean she wasn't the killer. She wouldn't return to the scene of her crime, would she? Then again, many killers do.

"Sammy, would you get the door? Hopefully it's the

sugar delivery," Libby called out to me from behind the bakery counter.

"Got it!" I rushed to the door and opened it, expecting to find a sweet delivery. Instead it was sour.

"Sammy, what a pleasant surprise! I'm here to talk to Libby, but I'd love to chat with you afterward." Winston smiled, but the look in his eyes was anything but friendly. His stare was intense as if he were staring down his prey.

"She's busy and so am I. Bye, Winston." I started to close the door but Winston stuck his foot over the threshold.

"Libby will want to talk to me." Winston dropped the smile.

"I'm busy right now, Winston, and I have nothing more to say about poor Griffin's death." Libby stood next to me.

"I see you're getting to ready to reopen the café. With Griffin dead, you'll get to keep your lease."

"Libby had nothing to do with Griffin's death." I stared at Winston. I tried to close the door but Winston's foot didn't budge.

Libby stepped in front of me and wagged a finger in Winston's face. "As I said earlier, I had nothing to do with Griffin's death. Stop making innuendos about me."

"As a reporter, I have to ask the hard questions, Libby." Winston took out his phone and opened up a text file. "Apparently Griffin wasn't the first person to try and take your lease out from under you. Does Joey Albright ring a bell?"

"You know it does," Libby snapped. "Yes, he tried to outbid me for this space. He complained and made false accusations against me. *Unfounded* accusations."

"So you deny running him out of town? Okay, fine. But unlike Joey, Griffin had a persistent real estate agent in Caleb. Were you ready to battle both of them?"

I put my arm around Libby's shoulders. Her face was red and her body shook slightly. I needed to get her away from Winston before this situation grew worse.

"That's enough, Winston!" I pushed the door harder and managed to move Winston's foot. Before the door slammed shut, Winston shouted, "I've got information you'll want, Sammy,"

I rested my forehead against the door and sighed. Winston obviously knew my weakness when it came to information. As much as I didn't want to take the bait, I had to. Libby didn't look angry anymore, but stressed.

"I'll go talk to him. You go back to work." I hugged Libby and then opened the door just wide enough for me to slide out. I pulled the door closed behind me but didn't move until I heard the lock click.

Winston leaned up against a streetlight, with a smirk on his face and his hat in his hand. "You couldn't resist me, could you?"

I laughed mirthlessly. "Don't flatter yourself. I'll listen to you for no more than five minutes."

"All business, then? Fine." Winston dropped the charming act. "Have you talked to Tessa? She won't return my calls, and her bodyguard of a roommate won't let me into their place."

"She's fine." I wasn't about to give him more information than that. Tessa obviously didn't want him to know anything if she didn't want to talk to him.

"Come on, I know you went to see her yesterday. What did she say about Griffin's death?"

"You don't care about Tessa, do you? You just want a sound bite from her for your blog."

Winston jerked his head back as if he had been hit.

"Wow, you must really think I'm some lowlife. I actually care about Tessa. We dated for a long time, and even though we're not together, I still love her."

I managed not to blurt out a snarky remark. Winston hadn't earned my trust, so I couldn't take his word at face value. But there was a sincerity in his voice that I hadn't heard before.

"I'm sure when she's ready to talk, she'll take your call," I said. "Besides asking about Tessa, what did you want to tell me? You have some important news to share?"

"I hope Tessa will." Winston put his hat on. "I thought you should know the word around the police department is that Griffin was poisoned with cyanide. Does Libby have access to that? Maybe in her paints?"

"Do you have access to cyanide?" Any goodwill I felt for Winston dissipated instantly. "How about Caleb?"

"Neither Caleb nor I made the poisoned latte." Winston narrowed his eyes. "Libby made the coffees. She's suspect number one in my book."

Actually Tessa had made the drinks, but I knew Libby wouldn't want me to tell Winston. He'd find out sooner or later, but not from me. He wouldn't get any information from me.

"Winston, if you're the journalist you claim to be, you shouldn't be throwing around accusations without any proof." I turned to leave, but Winston's voice made me turn back around.

"I am a journalist, unlike you. Sammy, you're just a nosy woman trying to protect her friends." Winston's voice was stone cold. "You got lucky a few times and helped your friends, but don't plan to this time. I'll find the killer first."

Winston crossed the street. He ignored the blaring horn

from the car that almost hit him and continued to the other side. The people on the sidewalk made room for him as he marched down the street. I didn't doubt Winston would do his best to find the killer. Or at least pretend to if he was the murderer.

19

Libby was in good hands with her employees, so I left the café. I called Andrew to see how everything was at Lagniappe Books.

"Enjoy the rest of the afternoon. You've been busy helping Libby, so take some time for yourself," he said.

"Are you sure? I wouldn't mind a walk in the sun. The temperature is a balmy sixty-two degrees."

Andrew's warm laugh came through the phone, loud and clear. "You are definitely a New Orleanian now. When I lived in New York, sixty-two degrees would have been lovely in November. People here act like this is blizzard weather."

"Oh, do you miss the cold and snow? I'm sure Beau would love to go skiing with you."

"I can hear you rolling your eyes over the phone." He snickered. "You know as well as I do, Beau will never set foot in the snow. I guess I'm a New Orleanian, too, since I have no desire to go anywhere cold ever again."

"I'll enjoy the weather for you, then. Thanks for holding down the fort."

We hung up, and I went to Jackson Square. I needed a

distraction from Griffin's murder, and the square was the perfect place to forget about it.

No matter the season, Jackson Square was undoubtedly the number one destination for tourists. On my first trip to New Orleans, I came here. I took a selfie in front of the gates to the park area of the square and sent it to my San Franciscan best friend, Madeline. After I moved here, Madeline framed the picture and sent it to me as a housewarming gift. "I call it *Samantha's New Beginning*. When things get tough, remember the joy and excitement of that moment," she said.

From Royal Street I turned down Pirate's Alley. The cobblestone path ran in between St. Louis Cathedral and the Cabildo. A shortcut to Jackson Square, the alley was lined with stores and a bar on one side. I stopped at Pirate's Alley Café and got a cocktail to go. Being able to take a drink out of a bar and walk around with it was still a novelty to me. I ordered my favorite drink, a Pimm's Cup, instead of one of the bar's famous absinthe drinks. After trying absinthe once, I avoid it since it has a hint of black licorice flavor which I hate.

I took my Pimm's Cup, a simple cocktail of Pimm's syrup, lemonade, and a splash of lemon soda, with me as I walked toward the black iron gates of the park area of the square. A crowd had formed around a ten-piece brass band clapping along to the bouncy music. Psychics offered tarot card and palm readings from surrounding tables. I weaved in and out of the tables until a hand grabbed mine.

"Hey! Oh, hi, Sutton." I recognized him from the clattering of turquoise bangles on his wrist. They matched his turquoise necklace. Even in the colder weather, Sutton O'Berry still wore his white linen shirt unbuttoned to his belly button. He had given in to the cooler temperatures by wearing closed-toe shoes instead of his usual flip-flops.

"Sammy, darling, come sit down and talk to me." He let go of my hand and gestured to the empty folding chair across from him. In between us stood a circular table covered in a black tablecloth and purple scarves. A stack of tarot cards, a crystal ball, and a sign that said, Sutton O'Berry, Extraordinary Psychic, Tarot Card Reader, and Your Guide to the Spiritual World (Cash Preferred) lay on the table.

"Just for a minute. I'm meeting a friend soon." I sat down.

"You're always so busy. I don't need to read your palm to understand that about you." Sutton winked.

"I imagine you've been busy, too. There are lots of people out today."

Sutton picked up his deck of tarot cards and shuffled them. The back of the cards were a deep purple with a gold eye in the center. He fanned them onto the table, blew on them, then stacked them in a neat pile.

"I haven't been as busy as I'd like to be. Let me do a quick reading for you. It'll get people interested and they'll come over. Please, Sammy."

"I'm serious that I have to go soon. Why don't you just do one card?" I took a gulp of my drink and set it down by my feet. Sutton might drink it "accidentally" if I put it on the table. I learned my lesson the last time I sat in this chair.

Sutton and I became friends after I saved him from being murdered. He prefers to say we worked together on getting out of a precarious situation. He claims it was destiny, but I'm skeptical. But I found him amusing enough to let him read my cards from time to time.

I had to admit I enjoyed tarot card readings because it was up to me to decide how to interpret the cards. Since each card had multiple meanings depending if it was upside down or right side out, you could decide if it matched anything in your life. Naturally, the tarot card reader tells you what they believe the cards mean, but I didn't always agree with what Sutton said. During my last reading, he told me that the Eight of Cups card meant I would soon travel, and it would be to a cold climate. I had no intentions of traveling, especially somewhere cold. But I ended up going over to Magazine Street in the Garden District to try a new ice cream shop with Connor the next day.

"Shuffle the cards, and then place them back in my hands." Sutton handed me the cards.

"Here you go." I gave him the shuffled cards, and then he fanned them on the table.

"Before you pick a card, think of what answer you seek today. Once you have, select a card with your left hand. Remember, don't look at it."

I didn't need to think of a question. What I needed to know was who killed Griffin, but I didn't expect the cards to give me a name. But I'd ask anyway. I picked my card with my left hand and placed it in Sutton's outstretched one.

"Oh, this card represents good news!" Sutton smiled gleefully after he turned the tarot card over. On the bottom, it said, "Page of Wands." A young man wore leggings, a tunic, a long scarf, and a hat with a feather, and held a wood staff. The background behind the man was full of sand and a line of pyramids.

Should I interpret the card's meaning as a sign that Griffin's killer will be revealed soon? Unfortunately, I couldn't rely on a tarot card to give me an actual name.

"I'd prefer good news over bad news. What does the wood staff mean?" I asked.

"Do you see how it's taller than the page? It means he has more to learn, but his ambition will take him to where he needs to go." Sutton tapped on the card. "Did you ask something about the murder at Libby's café?"

"Did you read my mind?" I laughed. "Yes, I asked who was the killer."

Sutton sighed. "No, Sammy, you know the cards don't work that way. I can enter a trance and visit the spiritual world, if you're interested. Let me find the dead man and ask him."

I shook my head as I didn't believe he could do that, but also I was aware of what would happen next.

"Since you're a friend, I can offer you a discounted rate on that service." Sutton perked up, but only for a minute after he saw my frown. "Okay, you're not going to go for that. So let's stick with this card. You are on the path to knowledge, so keep working toward your goal."

"Thanks. I will."

"By the way, have the police said what killed him? I heard it was cyanide poisoning. That is such a horrible way to die." Sutton ran a hand through his curly brown hair that turned grayer as the months passed.

"They haven't confirmed anything, but my guess is it was cyanide."

"So you smelled bitter almonds on his breath?"

"Um, yes. Did you hear about that, too?" I said.

"The grapevine is alive and well here in the Quarter," Sutton said. "I heard you were there, so I know you must have tried to help that man."

"I did, but how do you know about cyanide and the smell of bitter almonds?"

"I love Agatha Christie. Just like you do, I bet."

I didn't picture Sutton as a mystery reader, or frankly any kind of reader. "I do love her books. So you've read *Sparkling Cyanide*, then?"

"It's one of my favorites. The way the killer put the cyanide in the glass with no one noticing was shocking. Agatha was such a creative killer—in books, of course."

I agreed with Sutton. If only she were here to help me figure out Griffin's death. Before Sutton could offer to contact Agatha in the spirit world, I started to make my escape.

"Well, thanks for the reading, Sutton. I'd better run."

"You do know that cyanide is used to this day." Sutton touched his turquoise necklace. "My father made jewelry and used it for gold stripping. That makes the gold brighter."

"I had no idea about your father or about that use for cyanide. Thanks for sharing, Sutton."

"It's my pleasure to help you again, darling." Sutton reached over and grasped my hand. He kissed the top of it, which I wish he hadn't, as the smell of tobacco filled my nose. I removed my hand and stood up.

"Don't forget your drink unless you're done with it."

I picked up my drink, and before I could say anything, Sutton craned his neck as if he was looking around me.

"Ladies, I am finishing my session with this lovely client. I would then be delighted to read for each of you. You must have felt a connection to me since I'm from Texas, too."

I raised my eyebrows at Sutton, but didn't contradict his statement. Four young women wearing Texas A&M sweatshirts stood a few feet behind me. I had to give Sutton credit. He could connect with people right away. But I knew he grew up in Louisiana, not Texas.

The four girls giggled as they gripped their large to-go cups from the Daiquiri Den on Bourbon Street. Sutton could put on a show, but I wanted to make sure he didn't charge them more because of their tipsy status.

"Thank you, Mr. O'Berry, for that incredible reading. You are the best psychic here in Jackson Square and the best priced. Twenty dollars for a reading is such a great deal." I pushed myself up from the chair and opened my wallet. I handed him a twenty-dollar bill, plus a five as a tip. The college students might not know to tip him so I would help him with that part of the deal.

I leaned down as I handed him the cash and whispered, "You owe me beignets and coffee for helping you out."

He nodded and whispered, "Fine, but do I get to keep this money?"

I grinned and left his table. His reading wasn't worth twenty-five dollars, but his information about cyanide was.

20

I left Sutton and his new customers and went through the gates into the park. Tourists stood in line waiting to take their picture in front of the statue of General Andrew Jackson while others walked through the formal gardens and then out the gate on the Decatur Street side of the park. A circular pattern of metal benches surrounded the statue. I found an empty spot and sat down.

I listened to the brass band playing "When the Saints Go Marching In," and the crowd began singing and clapping along. I'd heard that song hundreds of times since I moved here, but I still liked it. Granted, I preferred to hear it only once a day as it took some time to get it out of my head.

Sutton's explanation of using cyanide in jewelry making got me thinking about where the poison came from for Griffin's murder. None of my suspects were jewelry makers, but they might have friends who are. I took out my phone and searched the internet for other sources of cyanide.

I had just started looking when I felt someone looking over my shoulder. I turned around to find Jasper standing behind me.

"I assume you're looking into the murder at the café and not planning one of your own." Jasper looked at me like a teacher catching a student goofing off in class. "Ruby couldn't have annoyed you that much today."

"No, I actually took part in her cleansing ceremony at Libby's earlier." I laughed along with Jasper. "What are you doing here in the park?"

"Let me come and sit with you for a bit." Jasper made his way around the bench and sat next to me. I'm sure we looked like an odd pair as he towered over me, even sitting down.

"I thought you'd be giving a tour or helping Beau with another plumbing problem," I said.

"Beau finally has a plumber on retainer, so I don't have to fix toilets or showers for him."

Jasper was a jack-of-all-trades when it came to construction, so he helped Beau at the Hotel Jeanne. There always seemed to be something to be fixed at the hotel. Beau claimed the ghosts were the ones causing problems. According to Jasper, the hotel's lack of maintenance by the previous owner and its old age were to blame.

"That's good." I wasn't sure it was actually a good thing, since Jasper was trying to save money to go to college. He didn't have the opportunity to go when he lived at home with his parents. Now that he was here, he wanted to study history even though he joked he'd be the oldest student at thirty-two.

"I prefer giving tours while I wait to hear from Tulane." Jasper worked with Neal, and the two were a great team.

"I'm so glad you applied." It took some convincing from me and Andrew to get him to do that. Jasper thought he should go to community college first, but we suggested he apply to Tulane. Even though Andrew worked there, he couldn't pull any strings for Jasper. But he helped him with his application.

And I wanted to help him with the financial side of going to school. This seemed like a good time to bring it up once again.

"Jasper, I was serious about using my brother's money for your education. I believe he would have wanted that. Just say the word and we'll go turn in those chips."

My brother had left a box of Biloxi casino chips in our family tomb for me. I had turned them in to the police, but Rob returned them to me soon after. The box sat on a shelf in my bedroom closet, waiting for me to make a decision. I didn't need the money, as my adopted parents left me a considerable inheritance after they died in a car crash. Most of the money I used to pay for my partnership in Lagniappe books, but I still had a decent chunk left in a retirement fund. My parents would have been proud of my practical use of their money.

"You're too kind, Sammy." Jasper put his arm around me and gave me a squeeze. "Let's hold off on that until I see what financial aid I get. You should use that money for yourself. Why don't you put it toward getting a detective license?"

Jasper grinned as I elbowed him in the stomach. "Ha, ha. I'm happy being a bookshop owner, thank you very much."

"Sure you are, but you are searching the internet for cyanide." Jasper pointed to my cell phone in my hand. "Any luck finding out how that guy was killed?"

I sighed. "No, I haven't. I don't know if the police have either. Rob and Christine are tight-lipped about this crime."

"You'll figure it out. You did with Hannah's death." Jasper rubbed his crescent-moon scar on his chin. The tragedy of Hannah's murder would never disappear entirely for him, but each day he got a little better. I didn't want to upset him, so I tried to change the subject.

"It'll work out. So tell me about your latest tour."

"Sammy, I can talk about the murder at Libby's. Really, it's okay." Jasper smiled, but there still was a sadness in his eyes. "You're looking up cyanide, so I guess that's what killed Griffin Blackthorn."

"I think so. Sutton just told me it's used in jewelry making, so I wondered what other uses it had."

"Besides murder? Actually, you use it to kill insects. My father and I used it on the farm to kill bugs around the barn. We kept it away from the cotton, though," Jasper said.

"I just read that it's used that way, but also in photography," I said. "That doesn't look good for Tessa, I'm afraid."

"Tessa doesn't seem like a killer." Jasper shook his head. "Your other suspects must have access to it."

I closed my eyes as if that would make my brain work harder. Winston must know people who use it, since he's a journalist. I wasn't sure if Suzy or Griffin knew anyone who had access to cyanide. But if Griffin wasn't the intended victim, he could have been the one who sourced the cyanide. As an art professor, he must have had access to all the supplies for the department.

"Earth to Sammy. Are you using your little gray cells like Poirot?" Jasper nudged me.

"Sorry, I guess I was." I laughed. "Since when do you know about Agatha Christie's Poirot?"

"Momma was telling me all about him the last time I talked to her. She said she's reading mysteries since you like them."

"That is so sweet of her." A warmth radiated through my body at Aunt Charlene's sweet gesture of reading books to connect with me. At times, I found her overbearing, but I always knew she meant well.

"Momma loves you. But not enough to dress up like Miss Marple for a costume party for your birthday. She said she doesn't want to look old." Jasper grinned.

"Please, no costume party for my birthday. Can't we just have cake?" I didn't mind a birthday party, but I just wanted something simple. But if Aunt Charlene was planning it, I might not have a choice.

"I'm reeling Momma in, trust me. I refuse to grow a handlebar mustache like Poirot. It's almost time for me to give a tour, so I need to go wait outside St. Louis Cathedral for our customers." Jasper stood up.

"I'm glad you found me here." I hugged Jasper. "Now, really, please think about using my brother's money. We can take a trip to Biloxi and cash the chips in together."

"You could use them at the blackjack tables instead of gambling on me."

"You're not a gamble, Jasper." I stepped back from our embrace so I could look him in the eyes. "You're a sure thing. I'd bet on you every time."

Jasper hugged me again before leaving for his tour. I sat on the bench and tilted my head back to look at the wispy clouds in the bright blue sky. I loved New Orleans for its history, music, culture, and food. But I absolutely loved it for the family it gave me.

As much as I wanted to grab another Pimm's Cup and go listen to more musicians on Royal Street, I didn't. It was time to head home and delve deeper into cyanide research. My laptop would be easier to use than my phone for that task. I just hoped it would produce more answers than questions.

21

———

I returned home to Nubi and my laptop. He curled up next to me as I sat on my sofa, clicking away at website after website. I confirmed that cyanide was used in photography, fumigation, and metallurgy. My suspects and Griffin could have obtained the poison through any of those sources. But I still was no closer to where the poison came from, who used it, and how they used it.

Connor came home with pizza for dinner, so I decided to forgo my investigation for the evening. A bottle of wine and pizza with my boyfriend was just the antidote to my frustration over my lack of progress in Griffin's murder. Although, our usual sparring over pizza choices made for a rocky start.

"I brought home a pepperoni pizza for me and a Hawaiian pizza for you." Connor put the pizzas on the stove. "You know how much I love you since I embarrassed myself for ordering it. I'll say it again: pineapple does not belong on pizza."

"Oh, no, Connor, the foodie was embarrassed." I put my hand up to my forehead dramatically. "Will his reputation continue to be sullied by his girlfriend's excellent choice in pizza toppings?"

"You are delusional if you think you know what is good on pizzas." He turned to Nubi, who had jumped on the counter and was sniffing the boxes. "I bet Nubi agrees with me."

Connor opened both boxes and picked up Nubi. "Which one is the right pizza, little guy?"

Nubi meowed when Connor showed him the Hawaiian pizza, but made no sound at the pepperoni pizza. He jumped out of Connor's arms and strolled to his dish and crunched on his dry food.

"Nubi doesn't know any better since you're his momma." Connor shook his head.

"He's a smart cat like his momma." I grinned. "Now let's just eat our own preferred pizzas and watch a movie. I'll even let you pick."

"Fine. But no complaining about what show I pick." Connor took out plates and wineglasses. "Not that I don't have excellent taste when it comes to movies."

He winked and opened the bottle of Merlot as I put the pizza slices on the plates. Fortunately, he did have excellent taste in movies and put on a British show. While it was a murder mystery movie, at least it differed from Griffin's death. A night snuggling up on the couch with Connor and Nubi while indulging in my favorite pizza and wine was just what I needed to forget about the real murder in my life.

"I'm going to kill him!" Connor slapped his hands on my kitchen counter, making my laptop pop into the air. "How could he do this to Momma?"

Connor's cell phone had beeped at 4:30 a.m. this morning, waking him, me, and Nubi. Typically, he turned the ringer off, but since Griffin's death, he had kept it on twenty-four seven. When he grabbed his phone, I assumed Libby had texted. Her plan was to arrive at the bakery at five, ready to prep for her opening day. Instead, a friend of Connor's texted a link to an article on Winston's blog.

We rushed to the kitchen and opened my laptop to find an article entitled "Are They Serving Murder at Artistic Coffee & Creations?"

Connor read it out loud. "The authorities have now labeled the suspicious death of artist Griffin Blackthorn as a murder. Sources at NOPD have confirmed that Mr. Blackthorn was poisoned with cyanide. Should Libby Tyler reopen her café, considering the victim drank a latte made by her? Rumor has it she is today, but do the police know? They must, since she is friends with the detectives on the case. Between Mrs. Tyler's close relationships with city officials and her community of protective and persistent people, will justice be served for Griffin? Or will his murder go unpunished?"

"You have got to be kidding me!" I pushed Connor over to read the rest of the article. "As a seasoned reporter, I am committed to uncovering the truth, even if the authorities won't. For full disclosure, Griffin Blackthorn was a close friend of mine. Our personal relationship will not cloud my judgment as I search for the café killer."

Connor stomped into the bedroom and got dressed. I did the same. We needed to get to Libby before she read the article. And I needed to keep Connor from tracking down Winston. I had never seen him this furious, and I wanted to keep him from doing something stupid.

I wanted to be the one to confront Winston. Did our

conversation yesterday push him to write such a scathing piece on Libby? My concern must have shown because Connor pulled me onto the sofa and said, "Sammy, don't blame yourself for that article. Winston would have said it even if you had been nice to him. We hate each other, so I'm sure that hasn't helped the situation."

I brushed his hair out of his face and placed my hand on his cheek. "Thanks, but I still feel bad about it, just like you do. I wanted to protect your mom. Instead, Winston has made things even harder for her."

"The Tylers are tough, so we'll get through this." Connor grasped my hand and kissed it. "Winston was right. We have friends here, but they'll do their jobs the right way. Not like that jerk."

A soft knock at my door startled us. Connor jumped up and checked the peephole. He swung the door open. "Oh, Momma, you heard, didn't you?"

The energy and hopefulness Libby had yesterday disappeared. Her eyes were red, contrasting with her pale face. "Your dad texted me about the article. He has an alert set up so he'll get notices if the café is mentioned anywhere online."

Connor ushered his mom into the apartment and over to the sofa. I hugged her and felt her gulp back a sob. "Libby, I'm so sorry. Winston is such a..."

Connor finished my sentence with an expletive, which his mother reprimanded him for making.

"Honey, we don't talk like that. It won't help and neither will you going to see him." Libby stood up and grasped Connor's hands. "There's no point in confronting Winston."

"Are you sure, Momma? You could sue him for libel. Let me call our lawyer."

Libby shook her head. "We're not bringing in lawyers. I

had a good cry over this, but I will not let it get to me. Or at least I'm going to try."

"I got my strength from you." Connor hugged his mom. "Let me cancel my plans for today so I can come to the café with you."

"No, darling. You can't let the kids down," Libby said.

Connor and a group of musicians arranged a music program at elementary schools to encourage kids to play music. They focused on schools outside of New Orleans, and they were supposed to visit schools in Baton Rouge today. They were leaving at 6:30 a.m. to beat the traffic.

"I'll be with your mom this morning until it's time to open my shop. Sissy is off today, so I'll message her to come stay with your mom."

"I appreciate y'all worrying about me, but I'll be fine," Libby said. "You don't need to call Sissy or anyone else to babysit me."

"Sorry, Momma, but you know I'm going to worry about you no matter what you say."

"Me, too," I said.

Libby wiped a tear from her face. "I love you two so much. But go on with your day, Connor. Between Sammy and the crew at the café, I'll be surrounded by love. If nobody comes to the café, we'll just eat the pastries ourselves."

Connor agreed not to cancel his program, but insisted on walking Libby and me to the café. We didn't talk as we walked through the quiet streets of the Quarter. At this early hour, only a few other people were outside, dressed in outfits that suggested they were heading to restaurants or bakeries. Most waved to Libby but kept on their way. Libby's purposeful stride with her head held high didn't offer anyone an opportunity to stop and talk with her, even if they wanted to.

"Now, honey, you go and do a great job with those kids today. I love you." Libby kissed Connor on the cheek and unlocked the bakery door. "I'll be in here when you're done saying your goodbyes."

"Bye, Momma. Love you." Connor smiled at his mother, but once the door closed, he stopped.

"Don't worry, I'll take care of her." I hugged Connor. "I've had my share of being accused of things I haven't done, so I can handle this."

Unfortunately, I had been accused of murder before and so had some of my friends and family. I believed I could help Libby deal with the fallout from Winston's article. Her strength and determination were strong this morning, so I didn't expect I'd have to do much to help her.

I was wrong.

Soft crying filled the empty café. I locked the door and joined Libby at a table. I took a pack of tissues from my little blue backpack and handed it to her. Libby pulled a tissue out and blotted the tears from her cheeks.

"Thanks, darling. I tried not to cry, but once I entered this place, I couldn't hold back. I don't want to lose my café." Libby blew her nose.

"You can't hold everything in all the time, Libby. A good cry always helps me."

"There is something about letting it all out, isn't there?" Libby smiled through her tears. "I didn't want to worry Connor, but I'm afraid Winston's article might keep people away from the café. I'll be fine financially because of William, but my employees depend on me. And then there are the artists I promote here."

"Let's take it one step at a time." I took in a deep breath

to calm my nerves. As a business owner, I grasped Libby's concerns, even though I hadn't hired any employees yet. Libby took her work seriously and the effects its loss would have on her staff and the community. "What do you want to do first? Besides, make me a café au lait?"

Libby laughed and pushed back her chair. "Let's get the coffee going and start baking. Are you ready to make your favorite scones?"

"You're going to let me see your family recipe?" I followed Libby behind the counter.

"It's about time you learned how to bake. I know Connor is teaching you how to cook, but baking is my domain." Libby pulled out a bag of coffee beans. "Coffee first, and then we'll start on the sweet potato scones."

Libby began making our drinks, otherwise I would have hugged her. I loved the scones, but the fact Libby wanted to share this family recipe with me meant the world. Hopefully I'd be better at baking than cooking. If nothing else, this was a perfect distraction from Winston's article and the potential fallout from it today.

22

———————

After a few sips of our steaming café au laits, Libby began teaching me how to make her famous scones.

"Now, first, I need you to take the brown butter out of the refrigerator. That's the secret to the rich taste of my scones," Libby said.

I opened the door to the industrial refrigerator and looked for boxes of butter labeled brown butter. "Libby, I don't see it."

She came over and grabbed a container from the top shelf. "Sorry, the label was on the other side."

"Brown butter comes in a plastic tub, not sticks?" I asked.

Libby giggled. "Sorry, darling, I keep forgetting you're not too familiar with baking and cooking. Brown butter is when you take butter and melt it until it's a pleasant shade of brown. It has a nuttier and bolder flavor than plain butter."

I should have felt embarrassed, but Libby's kind tone and patience as we worked together prevented that. She laughed along with me as I made noises while trying to work the dough into a ball. I started working on it before she said to put flour on my hands, so I was a sticky mess.

But when it was all said and done, and the scones were in the oven, I had to admit it was fun. But I would have been a wreck if I had done this alone.

"Libby, thanks for sharing the recipe with me. I'm honored."

"Honey, you're family, so I'm happy to share this with you." Libby smiled. "And you're not just family because of Connor. The day you walked into this café, I knew you were going to be part of my life."

Tears welled up in my eyes, but before I could thank Libby for her kindness, there was a loud knock at the front door. I ran to it, my stomach tossing at the possibility of the media, or worse, Winston, asking for a comment from Libby. My fears turned to relief as Libby's staff stood outside the door.

"Good morning, Sammy!" Mike stepped through the door. "I smell cinnamon, so you must be helping Libby with the sweet potato scones."

"Considering my lack of baking skills, I'm not certain if 'helping' is the appropriate term."

"Oh my, everyone is here! Y'all didn't have to come this early, but I'm glad you did." Libby wiped her hands on her apron as she trotted out from the kitchen. As she embraced everyone, I shut the door and heard a faint voice from the sidewalk.

"Sammy, it's me, Tessa. I'm not sure if I should come in." Tessa rubbed her arms as if she was trying to keep warm. She looked better than the other day, but the sadness in her eyes remained.

"Of course you should come in. Libby wants you here." I

didn't know that for a fact, but I doubted Libby would turn Tessa away.

"That's what everyone else said. They've been so nice. But with that article that jerk Winston wrote, Libby might not want me here."

"I would call him more than a jerk." I felt my anger rising, but that wouldn't help anyone right now. "Can you think of why he'd attack Libby? I hate to bring this up, but you know she didn't make the coffees."

Tessa squeezed her eyes shut and rubbed her arms even harder.

"Tessa, I'm not accusing you of anything." Well, I was, but I wouldn't get her to talk if I accused her outright.

"People must think I did it since I made the lattes, but I swear I didn't poison Griffin." Tessa opened her eyes. "I'll talk to Winston and make him change the article. If he thought not naming me would get me to talk to him, he's wrong."

"He wants to be in your life again..."

"Winston's a lot of things, but he's not a killer. He wouldn't kill anyone for me," Tessa insisted. "There was no reason to kill Suzy or Griffin for me."

I had doubts, but couldn't ask her any more questions. Pushing past me at the door, Libby took hold of Tessa's hand. She pulled her into the café.

"Tessa, I am so happy you're here!" Libby hugged her like she hadn't seen her in decades.

"I wasn't sure you'd want to see me after Winston's horrible article today." Tessa stared at the ground.

"Don't you worry about that man or what he says. You had nothing to do with Griffin's death." Libby put her arm around Tessa. "Now let's go inside and get ready for the day. Assuming you want to work."

"Um, could I work in the kitchen? I'm not ready to see people yet."

"Of course, darling. Come with me." Libby led Tessa to the kitchen, chatting away about the day's menu.

The entire crew prepared for the day as if it were any other day. I hoped it would be for Libby's sake.

At 7:30 a.m., Libby unlocked the front door. The tantalizing smell of the sweet and savory pastries and freshly brewed chicory coffee wafted through the café. As much as I loved the smells, I couldn't eat or drink right now. I worried the café would either be empty or filled with the media and true crime enthusiasts.

I had nothing to fear. Waiting outside the door were Libby's regular customers. Mr. Haywood, the gardener at St. Louis Cathedral, was first in line with a smile on his face. "Libby! I'm so glad you're open. I need my scone fix."

Person after person said similar things as they passed Libby. Andrew, Neal, and Jasper brought up the rear of the line.

"Y'all are here way too early!" Libby kissed each one as they came inside. "Sorry, but I better get behind the counter."

Libby dashed behind the counter and helped with orders. I noticed she didn't go near the espresso machine. I couldn't tell if it was deliberate or just how things were unfolding. I chatted with my friends as they waited in line.

"Connor texted us about the outrageous article in that distasteful blog." Andrew pulled down the cuffs of his shirt. "We wanted to be here in case she needed help."

"Or protection. If anyone bothers Libby, we're on it.

Right, Jasper?" Neal elbowed Jasper, who stared at his cell phone.

"Oh, yeah, of course." Jasper looked up from his phone but went back to it. "Listen to this in the actual newspaper. 'Detective Christine Gammon confirms that artist Griffin Blackthorn died from cyanide poisoning. The investigation is ongoing and we have not confirmed any suspects at this time.' That sounds more credible than Winston's supposed reporting."

"Speak of the devil." Neal pointed to the door where Winston stood outside.

"Oh no! He's not bothering Libby this morning." I started toward the door, but Jasper grabbed my arm.

"Sammy, remember, he might be a killer. Don't go anywhere with him. Actually, we should all go outside with you," Jasper said.

"He won't talk to me if y'all are with me." I gently took my arm away from Jasper. "But I promise not to go anywhere with him."

"We'll be watching and waiting, then." Andrew gestured for Neal and Jasper to move up to the counter. "Sammy can take care of herself, and we should talk to Libby."

"And order food. I'm starving." Neal and Jasper placed their orders.

"Be careful, though. I don't trust that man." Andrew glared at Winston, who opened the door.

I nodded and then rushed to the door. Winston looked startled as I blocked the doorway.

"Sammy, are you in line? I promise I'm not trying to cut ahead of you." Winston's voice oozed with confidence and humor, but it didn't work on me.

I closed the door behind me and pointed toward a hitching post. "Let's talk over there."

Winston looked back and forth between me at the post and the café's door. He finally came over to me.

"All right, Sammy. I guess you want to talk to me about my article last night." Winston sighed. "I find it hard to believe that you weren't aware of that information from your sources."

"Come on, you know I'm here to talk about your allegations against Libby. Why are you targeting her? She didn't make the lattes. Tessa did."

"Really?" Winston took off his hat and clutched the rim with both hands.

"Yes." The other day I didn't want to throw Tessa under the bus, but my loyalties were with Libby. I couldn't let a lie ruin her business.

"Oh. I was told Libby made the drinks."

"Who told you?"

Winston shoved his hat on and inhaled deeply. "I can't tell you. My source asked to remain anonymous."

"I'd rethink using your source, then. He or she doesn't know what they're talking about."

"I've got to go, but tell Libby if she wants to tell her side of the story, I'm all ears."

He hurried away from me, ignoring my calls to come back. I had more questions for him, but they'd have to wait. Who was Winston's source? Could Tessa, Suzy, or Caleb be the one? Winston might have fabricated having a source. Who would want to throw suspicion on Libby?

The killer.

Andrew, Neal, and Jasper waited for me at a table near the front window. They had watched my conversation with

Winston, but couldn't hear what we had said. I took a sip of the café au lait they had ordered for me, before speaking.

"Winston claims an anonymous source told him Libby made the lattes. I told him it was Tessa. He genuinely seemed surprised," I said. "Then again, he could be acting."

"He could be, especially if he's the killer. Can you imagine writing about the murder that you committed?" Neal said.

"Samantha can—"

Neal interrupted Andrew. "What do you mean?"

"He means I've read enough books to know that killers write about their crimes. Both in fiction and nonfiction books," I said.

"Don't worry, Neal. Sammy only solves crimes." Jasper picked up a chocolate chip cookie from his plate. "Like who stole my other chocolate chip cookie."

"Now, that one's easy." I pointed at Neal. "He has a blueberry muffin on his plate, but a smear of chocolate on his chin. Neal is your culprit."

If only Griffin's murder was as easy to solve as the case of the missing cookie.

23

Today was normally an administrative day for me, so Andrew insisted I work from the café. With my laptop and a continuous supply of coffee and pastries, I kept an eye on Libby and the café. I texted Connor with updates about his mom. He thanked me for spending the day with Libby, but she hadn't needed me.

The reopening day went without a hitch. A few true-crime fans came in but didn't make a scene. Most of them left quickly after they realized there was no evidence of Griffin's death. An art dealer came by looking for Griffin's paintings, so Libby referred him to Suzy.

"What a day! I can't thank y'all enough for your hard work." Libby and her employees sat in the café, including Tessa. After hours in the kitchen, she stepped out for the first time. Libby had Tessa sit next to her and included her in the group's conversation. Tessa wasn't fully engaged, as Libby had to call her name twice to get her to answer.

"I don't know what tomorrow will be like, but let's get back to our regular schedule." Libby opened a folder on the table and pulled out the employee schedule. I took the opportunity to leave, since William was back in town and would walk Libby home.

"You're such a doll. Thanks for helping me with everything today." Libby hugged me before I left. "I'm so lucky to have you."

It was just about 3:30 p.m. when I left the café. Connor and I had plans to go to Coop's for dinner when he returned from his school visit. My belly would rumble for fried chicken and jambalaya by the time he got home. Right now, I was full of sweet potato scones and café au lait.

Having a drink wasn't part of my afternoon plans, but running into Rose Herbert changed my mind.

"Hi, Rose! On your way to work?" I saw Rose on my way home to clean my apartment and do the laundry.

"I am. What are you up to?" Rose pushed up the sleeves of her baby-blue cardigan, revealing her latest tattoo. A delicate magnolia flower covered most of her forearm. As a bartender at The Gas Light, Rose handled any obnoxious patrons with one steely look and a raise of her pierced eyebrows. But her toughness didn't extend to her love of pastel sweaters and flower tattoos.

"I should go home and do chores, but I can't say I'm very motivated. Spending the day at the café wore me out."

"Then come to the bar with me, and you can tell me how Libby's doing and what you know about the murder. The first Pimm's Cup is on me."

By the time we reached the bar on Chartres Street, Rose knew everything I did.

"Wow, this is all bizarre. Do you think Griffin or Suzy was the intended victim?" Rose asked.

"Because of the cup switch, it seems like Suzy. But something just doesn't feel right."

I opened the door to the bar and let Rose walk in first.

The Gas Light had all the makings of a dive bar, with its barely noticeable sign by the door and lackluster interior. The mix of square and round wooden tables had seen better days. A long bar stretched the length of the room and was lined with wobbly stools. The lighting was dim from the gas lights on the right-hand-side wall. The Gas Light was not intended for tourists; rather, it catered to locals in search of a laid-back watering hole to drink with friends and neighbors. I'd take this bar over any fancy one.

"For Libby's sake, I hope it gets resolved soon. I'll go to the café tomorrow and offer my support." Rose headed to the back of the bar. "I'll bring your drink to you once I get settled in."

"Thanks. I'll go sit with the poker players."

Terry and Jimmy were deep into a poker game. The bowl of stale peanuts in the center of the table was almost empty. They used them as betting chips, and Terry had a bigger pile.

"Sammy, are you ready to play yet?" Jimmy dealt the cards to him and Terry.

"No, I still haven't learned how to play."

"Cher, you've got to get that boyfriend of yours to teach you." Terry sipped his beer.

"Better yet, get Miss Momo to teach you. She was the best player in the Quarter back in the nineties. I lost a lot of peanuts to her," Jimmy said.

"Momo? I had no idea she played." It didn't surprise me that Momo was a good card player. I met Myrtle "Momo" McBride, when she called me up to her balcony when I was walking to Beau's hotel. She and her cat, Lady Clementine, were both charming and entertaining. She'd become a friend that day. After helping her solve the mystery of her missing niece, we'd become even closer. As an octogenarian, she'd had many chapters in her life, so why not one as a poker player? With her petite frame and sweet smile, I bet she disarmed the other players when she beat them.

"She was as ruthless as a gator with an empty stomach. Momo would drink her bourbon, light a cigarette, and distract the other players with stories about her duck hunting trips and how to make the best potato salad." Terry grinned. "Before I knew it, she'd play her hand, and the rest of us would be dumbfounded that we didn't see it coming."

Rose dropped off my drink, and I sat and watched the two men play. Talking about Momo inspired them to distract each other. Terry called out to the guys at the table next to us, trying to get them to talk about the upcoming Saints game. They wouldn't talk after Jimmy yelled, "This old gator is trying to cheat! Don't help him."

I sipped my cocktail and tried to pay attention to the poker game. Focusing was hard because I kept thinking about Griffin, Suzy, Caleb, and Winston at the café table. The only plausible time one of them might have poisoned the coffee was during Libby's speech. If Terry and Jimmy couldn't distract each other enough to steal peanuts, how could a killer pour poison into a coffee mug without being seen? I wish I had watched their table the entire time, but no one expected a murder to occur.

Tessa at the espresso maker was something I couldn't get out of my mind. Is it possible that she poisoned the cup while making the lattes? Libby stood next to Tessa as she worked, but she might have been distracted. If Tessa was the killer, then her intended victim was Griffin. Since he was the only one with an almond milk latte, she couldn't control who would die if she poisoned the other three drinks. Unless she didn't care if she killed Suzy, Caleb, or Winston.

Did she have a strong enough motive to kill any of them, though?

Did any of them really have strong motives to kill one another? I considered going to track down all my suspects after I finished my drink. Libby had a successful reopening day, and I prayed it would continue. Having Griffin's murder solved would help toward that goal.

"Sammy, you look like you're a zillion miles away. Are you okay?" Terry asked.

"Yes. My mind is wandering. Whoa, I missed a lot of the game. Did you cheat, Terry?"

"I did not! Don't you go accusing me of stealing peanuts from Jimmy. He can't help it if he's a bad player." Terry pointed his empty beer bottle at me and then at Jimmy.

"You just got lucky this time," Jimmy said. "You should have let me win one round for helping you cart all those paintings to Libby's."

"I bought you a Lucky Dog. Wasn't that enough? I got you a drink, too." Terry laughed so hard his dentures popped out. He shoved them back in his mouth as Jimmy shook his head.

"Oh, yeah, a plain hot dog and a warm coke from a cart were *so* fancy."

I laughed at Jimmy's deadpan delivery. Lucky Dog carts could be found all throughout the French Quarter day and night. Sometimes a good old-fashioned hot dog and soda hit the spot, but I agreed with Jimmy. It wasn't a fancy meal.

"Terry, you owe him a meal at a sit-down restaurant. You should take him to Commander's Palace," I said. There would be no hot dogs and soda there, but turtle soup and martinis. And a big check at the end of the meal.

"Whoa, cher, you think I'm made of money? I haven't

sold any of my paintings yet." Terry gaped at me. "You want to buy the whole lot?"

"I thought the painting of me and Connor was a present when I got married. Now you're making me pay for my gift?" I feigned indignation.

"She's got your number." Jimmy roared with laughter. "While you calm down, I'll get our next round. Sammy, you need another drink?"

"No, thanks. I'm going to head home before I meet Connor for dinner. And no, we're not going to Commander's Palace."

"Good to see you." Jimmy smiled at me, then turned and frowned at Terry. "Don't you go marking those cards. I've got eyes in the back of my head."

"Then put those eyes in the front of your head so you can play better." Terry laughed as Jimmy ordered more beers from Rose behind the bar.

If I had eyes in the back of my head when Griffin was poisoned, I could have seen who put the cyanide in the coffee. But I hadn't, so it was up to good old-fashioned investigating to find the murderer.

24

───────

"**Y**ou're eating jambalaya for breakfast? I taught you how to make an omelet. Why not make one?" Connor asked over the phone.

"Because reheating leftovers is much easier than cooking a fancy omelet." I took my bowl out of the microwave and sat on my sofa. I had my cell phone on speakerphone, so I could listen to Connor's disappointment over my lack of cooking.

"I should have made breakfast before I left."

"That's a sweet thought, but there was no way I was getting up at five a.m. to eat an omelet, no matter how good it was."

Connor left my apartment this morning to go out of town for two nights. He had joined a new band, Bayou Brass Revelry, and his first performance with them was in Houston.

"I don't know. My omelets are world famous. Yeah, I'm coming, Mac." The sound of a car door slamming came through the cell phone. "Sorry, Sammy. Mac is yelling for us to get moving. I'll call you tonight. Love you."

"Love you, too." I ended the call and finished my jambalaya. No omelet I made could have matched the deliciousness of my leftovers. I might try making Libby's sweet potato scones now that I had the recipe and the baking lesson to go with it.

I had the day off from work, but I had no time to bake. My plan was to talk to all my suspects and try to narrow down whether Suzy or Griffin was the intended victim. Caleb's office was my first stop.

As a commercial real estate agent, I expected Caleb to have a flashy office close to the Central Business District. Instead, I found him in a small room in the outbuilding of a town house on the edge of the Quarter by the Marigny neighborhood. The main building housed a women's clothing store, but the side alley opened up to a courtyard with a one-story cottage in the back. One door had a For Rent sign. The other had a handwritten paper tacked to the door: "Caleb Rhodes, Real Estate and Business Developer." To the left of the door was a window with black curtains and a window box with dead plants.

I knocked on the door and heard shuffling and murmurs from inside. Caleb opened the door with a smile on his face, but it vanished abruptly.

"Sammy, what a surprise. How did you find me?" Caleb leaned up against the doorframe.

"Beau gave me your address."

Caleb had called the same day he met Beau, asking for a meeting. He wanted to meet Beau at his office, but Beau insisted on seeing his place. They set their meeting for the end of the next week. By the disarray that I could see around Caleb's office, he clearly wasn't ready for visitors.

"And to what do I owe the pleasure of your visit? Did

you think of any other cafés for sale?" The smile returned to Caleb's face.

"I'm still working on it. In the meantime, I thought we could talk about retail storefronts. Andrew and I are thinking of adding other locations of Lagniappe Books," I lied. Andrew and I were both happy with one shop. Caleb would be the last person I'd call, even if we wanted another location.

"That's fantastic! Let me grab my coat, and we can go somewhere to get coffee." Caleb stepped inside his office.

"I only have a little time, so let's chat here." I followed Caleb inside the office and understood immediately why he didn't want me to see the inside. To my right and in front of me were gray metal storage cabinets with dings and rust spots. Sagging cardboard boxes were up against the wall under the window. The only decent piece of furniture was the cherrywood executive desk with a brown leather high-back chair and a console table. Papers were scattered on the top of the desk as opposed to the neat piles of folders which were stacked on one end of the console table. A tray held two crystal glasses and three decanters. One bottle was empty, while the other two were half-full, with a brown liquid in one and a clear liquid in the other.

"You'll have to excuse the mess." Caleb stiffly pointed to the cabinets and boxes behind him. "The previous tenant didn't take all their things, and my landlord hasn't removed them yet."

"No worries. From the labels on the boxes, my guess is they're photographers." Two of the boxes were labeled developer supplies and film.

"Yes, this was their darkroom. Why don't you take a seat?"

I sat in the wingback chair facing the desk and glanced

at my watch. Not that I cared about the time, but I didn't want to get stuck here for too long. Unless, of course, Caleb provided information I needed about Griffin's death.

"Your desk and table are beautiful. Are these your pieces? The decanter set must be," I said.

Caleb relaxed as he sat in his chair. He rubbed his hands along the edge of the desk. "Yes, this is a family desk. Every Rhodes man has used it for their business, along with the decanter set. My great-grandfather said every deal should be closed with a drink."

"How nice you're keeping that tradition alive." I smiled, hoping to keep Caleb relaxed and chatty. "Did you have any luck finding a space for yourself? You really must miss the café business."

"I do. I miss talking with customers and having coffee whenever I needed it."

I laughed. "I understand the need for coffee. Do you have a name picked out? Tessa said it was called The Pines Café, but that won't work here."

"No, it won't." He shook his head. "Tessa must have been the one to tell you the name of the old place."

"She did. Would you hire her again? She's still in the business, although Winston isn't."

"I'd never hire Winston to do anything. He caused more trouble for us than he was worth. Tessa, too." Caleb sat up straight in his chair and moved the papers around his desk. My days as an administrative assistant taught me how to read upside down so I could see one paper was a letter from the Louisiana Real Estate Commission. It was reminding him to complete his required continuing education credits for the third time. Another was a bank statement with a zero balance in the account.

"I'm sorry to hear that, especially about Tessa. Libby raves about her."

"Libby won't listen to me after Griffin made her think I wanted her space for him." Caleb leaned back in his chair. "But tell her to keep an eye on Tessa. She wanted to be part of Griffin's and my gallery and cafe when we opened it here."

"Really?" I scooted my chair closer. From the spark in his eyes, I got the impression Caleb enjoyed sharing a bit of gossip. "Did she want to sell her photography along with Griffin's paintings?"

"Maybe, but I know she offered to run the café along with the art gallery. He wasn't so sure about it. Suzy and Tessa don't get along, so I don't know how that would have worked."

"So the café would have been you and Griffin with, possibly Tessa?" I said.

"Definitely Griffin and me, but I wasn't keen on Tessa's involvement. Suzy wouldn't have liked it. But that's neither here nor there. I'm on my own." Caleb sighed. "But let's talk about you. What kind of space do you need for another shop?"

Caleb wrote notes as I made up details about my fictional needs for more retail locations. Part of me felt bad for wasting his time, but if he turned out to be the killer, the time hadn't been wasted for me.

25

———

After promising to touch base with Caleb next week, I left his office. The pushy-salesman style he used when visiting businesses disappeared the longer we spoke. He genuinely had a good understanding of the real estate market in the French Quarter and appeared interested in my needs.

Winston was next on my list of suspects to visit. He didn't have an office that anyone knew of, so I assumed he worked from home. I heard he lived in the Bywater neighborhood, which was two neighborhoods over. Since his neighborhood was too big to go door to door looking for him, I needed his actual address.

Connor and Winston had worked together, so they had mutual friends, or rather, acquaintances in Winston's case. I really didn't want to ask Connor if he had a friend who knew his address, but if I had to, I would. Connor wouldn't want me to go to Winston's house by myself for two reasons. The first, he didn't trust Winston, and second, he would be worried that Winston could be the killer. But he loved his momma more than anything and would help me to solve this murder.

Before I called him, I decided to check on Libby and grab a coffee for my potential walk to Winston's house. The sun was shining, and the temperature was creeping upwards to the sixties. I'd take warm weather over the cold, so a walk sounded good to me.

But I didn't need to go all the way to the Bywater. Winston stood outside the café, fidgeting with his phone.

"Are you bothering Libby?" I snapped as I walked to him. I adjusted my tone, though, as I realized being snippy wouldn't get me answers. "Or do you need coffee and a scone?"

"I need coffee, but I was actually trying to get ahold of Tessa."

"She still isn't answering your texts or calls? Do you want me to get a message to her?"

Winston looked startled. "You'd help me? That's a first."

"Taking a message to her isn't a big deal. I can't guarantee she'd want to talk with you," I said.

"Oh, well, thanks. Could you just ask her to call me? Tell her it's business, not personal, if that will help."

"Business? If it's for your blog, I can't imagine she'd be too interested."

"Maybe not, but I don't want to say she made the lattes in my next article without talking to her." Winston shoved his phone in his pocket. "If I don't publish the truth, I'm not really a reporter. But this is hard since she's a friend."

For once, Winston truly seemed like a reporter who wanted to tell the truth. But he also seemed like a caring human being by the way he said how hard it would be to report on Tessa. The reporter in him won out.

"Tell her I'm writing an update article tonight, so please

call me before nine. Thanks, Sammy." Winston started to leave.

"Winston, wait up." I walked up next to him and he stopped. "Did you know Griffin and Caleb were going to open a café together again?"

"What? I'm surprised they wanted a repeat experience."

"Why do you say that?"

"Let's just say they weren't the best business partners, at least in my opinion. They had to close the café."

I nodded. "Tessa told me. Do you think she would work with them again?"

"I hope she'd know better than to trust Griffin." Winston scowled and changed the subject. "You're all nosy today. Not having any luck finding the killer?"

"Are you having any luck?" I plastered a fake smile on my face.

"Maybe."

I studied his face for any hint that he was holding back information. He didn't have the gleam in his eyes when he was excited about the news he had found. I couldn't be positive, but I didn't think he had any new information.

"Do you think Griffin or Suzy were the intended victim?" I decided to keep asking him questions since he did have more background on the suspects than I had. But I had to take into consideration that he could try to protect Tessa or himself, by lying to me.

"Good question. I'd say Suzy, since it was her original mug that was poisoned."

"Yes, but who would want to kill Suzy? Griffin seems like the most likely suspect."

"He does. I wouldn't be surprised if he drank too much from his flask and mixed up the mugs," Winston said.

"Do you think he was really drunk?"

"He didn't seem that way, but then again, he hid it well while he was teaching," Winston said.

"So you think Griffin was drunk and got confused?"

"I'm not committing to anything just yet. I'll tell you one thing and one thing only. I'm following the insurance trail. Money makes people do bad things."

But so does love. Winston tipped his hat and hurried away. I'd already followed the insurance trail, and Griffin and Suzy had reason to kill each other. Caleb had an insurance policy on Griffin; Griffin would have more money for a place in the Quarter if Suzy died.

To me, Caleb and Tessa had motives to kill Suzy. They also had motives to kill Griffin. Perhaps Caleb meant to kill Suzy, not only for the insurance money Griffin would receive, but to cause a scandal at the café. He might have thought Libby would close her business or the building owner wouldn't renew her lease. Griffin seemed to be putting a lot of pressure on Caleb to find a place for him. Would he have committed murder just for real estate?

Tessa's motive was the most obvious—revenge for leading her on, romantically. But she could have been trying to kill Suzy in order to have Griffin all to herself. No matter if Suzy or Griffin was the intended victim, Tessa had strong motives to kill both of them.

And then there was Winston. Is there a chance that he murdered Griffin to get Tessa back? The only reason I could think he'd want to kill Suzy was to frame Griffin. Did he love Tessa that much?

The café had returned to normal. All the tables were filled with customers drinking and eating. Some chatted with their table mates while others typed away on their laptops. Yesterday's reopening was the start of business as usual for Libby.

"Sammy, darling, isn't this wonderful?" Libby leaned over the counter and grasped my hands. "It's been such a relief to have everyone back."

"I'm so happy for you." I squeezed her hands. "Hopefully, you're not sold out of sweet potato scones."

"You have good timing. Tessa is bringing out a tray in just a moment. Do you want a café au lait to go with it?"

"You know me all too well."

"And I know you well enough to know that you're here for more than food. Do you need to talk to Tessa?"

"I do. If you don't mind."

"She's been pretty quiet, so it'll do her some good to talk to you."

Libby refused to let me pay and left to make my drink. I moved over to the coffee station to wait for my order. I couldn't believe just four days ago, I stood there and watched Griffin collapse. I closed my eyes, trying to picture the events of that night. How could someone manage to poison the coffee without anyone noticing? It had to be in those pink sugar packets. Rob and Christine would have to release more information sooner or later about the evidence, wouldn't they?

"Sammy, are you okay?"

I opened my eyes to find Tessa holding a coffee cup and a small pastry box. "Yes, just resting my eyes. Is that my order? Thanks."

Tessa handed me my café au lait and the box of scones. I inhaled the sweet smell of the warm scones and sighed. "I baked scones with Libby yesterday, but they didn't smell as good as these. Thank goodness Libby has you to bake and not me."

"Libby said you did a great job, so don't sell yourself short." Tessa smiled, but there was a sadness in her eyes.

"How are you? I imagine it's hard to be back here."

Tessa turned her head toward the table where Griffin and the group had sat on that fateful night. "I'm in the kitchen most of the time, so it's easier. Everyone has been nice, though."

"I'm glad to hear it. Listen, I hate to bother you about Winston, but..."

"But he asked you to have me call him," Tessa said. "Sorry he put you in the middle of us."

"He says he just wants to see how you're doing. But he mentioned he wanted to confirm some information from the night Griffin died."

Tessa pulled at the hem of her dress before answering me. "He must have found out I was the one who made the drinks, not Libby. I wanted to make him correct it, but Libby said it didn't matter."

While I was glad to hear Libby wasn't concerned with Winston's reporting any longer, I hated her being accused of murder in his blog.

"Winston said he wanted to report the correct information. He asked that you contact him before nine tonight."

"Okay, thanks for telling me. I'm sorry he's bothering you."

I placed a hand on Tessa's arm. "He'd probably say I'm bothering him, so don't worry."

"You're bothering him?" Tessa pulled her arm away from my hand. "Are you talking to everyone about Griffin's death? Did you come to see me just to ask me questions? Do you think I'm a killer?"

The surrounding tables turned their attention to us as Tessa's voice had grown louder.

"No, I don't, Tessa. And I really was concerned about you when I brought you lunch. I still am now." I lowered my voice and stepped away from the tables. Tessa didn't do the same as I hoped.

Tessa stomped away toward the kitchen without a word. My heart sank, knowing I'd offended her. Before all this had happened, I enjoyed talking with her about her photography. I'd even connected her with an artist collective. She used their darkroom when she did traditional photography instead of digital.

But if she turned out to be the killer, it wouldn't matter. Although I would care about Libby's reaction to having a killer on her staff. Libby prided herself on her ability to made a quick, and accurate, judgment of someone's character. I benefited from this ability since she rented my apartment to me on the basis of our first meeting at the café. And the fact I solved a mystery for her right then. I really needed to solve this mystery for her, too.

Libby frowned when I went to the counter. "What just happened, Samantha?"

"I passed along a message from Winston, but she's more upset with me." My face felt warm. "She doubted my sincerity. My concern for her is genuine."

"Of course it is, honey." Libby's face relaxed. "Tessa is still mourning, so she's not thinking clearly."

I nodded, and the heat on my face disappeared. But I shouldn't have relaxed.

"I'm not mourning like Tessa, but I do worry that the goodwill people are showing now will fade. Don't tell Connor or William that, though. If they think I have any doubts, they'll keep on me." Libby shook her head. "I love them dearly, but their constant pep talks are more stressful than helpful. I feel the need to hide my moments of doubt."

"Oh, Libby. I'm so sorry." I bit my lip so I wouldn't cry. She didn't need me stressing about her, at least not in front of her.

"Thanks, honey. I'll be fine." She patted my hand. "Thanks for letting me vent. Now, do you need anything else? More chocolate croissants are coming out in a minute or two."

"The scones are plenty, thanks. Let me know if you need any help, including wrangling Connor." I smiled.

"You love him, and that's all I need. Don't you worry about me. When Rob and Christine arrest the killer, I'll feel better. Everyone will."

I agreed, although, unlike Libby, I wasn't waiting for them to solve it.

26

L eaving Libby's café, I was even more determined to find the killer. Talking to Suzy was next on my list. I texted Andrew: *Have you seen Suzy at her shop?*

He called me back. "You could have called instead of texting."

"Sorry, it's just habit."

Andrew disliked texting but had embraced it as a necessary evil. But he would call rather than text more often than not.

"A bad habit, if I may say so."

"Yes, it's a bad habit. Are you calling me because Suzy is at her shop?"

"I am, but before you ask, I didn't text because it would take too long."

I blew out an exasperated sigh. I loved Andrew, but some days I wish he would get to the point quickly. "So, what's going on?"

"Suzy is at her shop. All three of your other suspects have been by to see her."

"What?" The one day I wasn't at the shop and this

happened.

"Tessa came by first when Suzy opened up. They talked for a few minutes. While they didn't hug goodbye, it seemed cordial."

"Wow! Who came next?"

"Winston went into the shop, but left with Suzy standing at the door, ushering him out. Fifteen minutes later, Caleb arrived and stayed for ten minutes. He left on his own."

"I see why you called me. Thanks for the information."

"You're welcome. If I'm going to be a spy, I might need a tuxedo."

"You would look fabulous in a tux. I'll talk to you later. Thanks."

"Signing off, Ballard, Andrew Ballard."

I put away my phone and headed to Suzy's shop. What in the world did everyone have to say to her?

The bell over the door chimed as I entered Suzy's Surprises. As usual, her 1950s' music playlist came through the speakers in the ceiling. The shop had no space for speakers anywhere else. Shelves from floor to ceiling lined three walls, filled with merchandise. From colorful music boxes to oyster-shell trinket dishes, Suzy offered unique gifts along with the standard souvenirs, like T-shirts and boxes of pralines. Between the music and merchandise, my senses were overloaded every time I came in here.

Suzy stood behind her sales counter at the back of the shop. A display of postcards sat next to the cash register. Did people still send postcards? I hadn't received any in years. My adopted parents mailed them to me when I first went away to college. It was a sweet gesture, but I wondered if it had been their way to remind me Florida was warm and sunny as opposed to foggy San Francisco.

Two tourists were making purchases. They bought four boxes of pralines, a bag of Mardi Gras beads, and fleur-de-lis-shaped candleholders.

"Now, y'all enjoy the rest of your trip here. And come back and see me if you decide you want T-shirts for your grandkids." Suzy handed the couple a large shopping bag, and they made their way out of the shop.

"Hi, Suzy. Glad to see you're open," I said.

"I don't want to sit around at home, so working keeps me busy." Suzy came out from behind the sales counter. Up close, I could see she had tried to cover up the circles under her eyes with makeup. Her trademark Cupid's bow lips were bright red, but the rest of her face was pale.

"How are you holding up?"

She gave a bitter laugh. "Can't you tell? I look horrible no matter how much makeup I put on."

"You look fantastic," I lied. "This is a terrible time for you."

"It just keeps getting worse. Everyone is visiting me and asking questions."

The pit in my stomach grew bigger as Suzy stared at me. I wasn't sure whether to leave or ask my questions.

"Don't worry, Sammy. I know you're here to ask questions, too." Suzy sighed. "Ask away."

"I'm sorry. I don't want to upset you, but I wonder if you were the intended victim. Who would want to hurt you?"

"I'd love to believe no one would want me dead, but someone poisoned my mug." Suzy picked up a T-shirt and refolded it. "So, as I told the detectives, Tessa is first on my list, for obvious reasons. She'd get Griffin all for herself. Now Winston might kill me to get Tessa back. "

"Why would he kill you and not Griffin?"

"To frame Griffin for my murder!" Suzy's tired eyes widened.

Winston didn't strike me as the type of person who would go the roundabout way to get rid of his supposed romantic rival. But I let Suzy continue without commenting out loud.

"Caleb's motive is money. Now that I know Griffin had more insurance on me than I was aware of, if I died, Griffin would have plenty of funds to buy and run a café with Caleb."

I had to give Suzy credit for having those motives figured out. I agreed with her, assuming she was the intended victim. But what if Griffin was really the target? Suzy had thought of that, too.

"Now, of course, if someone wanted to kill Griffin, all those motives I mentioned would still work. Tessa was angry Griffin wouldn't leave me, and Winston hated Griffin. Caleb must have insurance on Griffin for their business."

"You've thought a lot about this," I said.

"The detectives did. And all those people I mentioned. They all came by today to check on me. So they claimed."

"That's strange, isn't it? I didn't realize you were close to any of them."

"No, I'm not. Tessa claimed she wanted to let bygones be bygones."

"Did you believe her?"

"To be honest, yes, I did." Suzy sounded sincere. "I have no plans to become friends with her, but it won't help me to hold on to any anger toward her."

Suzy's sudden generosity of spirit surprised me after the interactions I saw between her and Tessa. I hoped she meant it, but my suspicious mind now wondered if the two of them worked together to kill Griffin. Not that there was any proof, but I'd read enough psychological thrillers to know that could happen. Well, at least in fiction.

"Do you feel the same about Winston?"

"Winston is annoying, to say the least, but at least he's honest about his motives. He asked if I would do an interview about Griffin's death. Having an exclusive interview with me would help him, he admitted."

"Did you say yes?"

Suzy shook her head. "I said no and shooed him out of the shop. Caleb arrived after him, but I consider him more of a friend than the others, certainly."

"Oh, I assumed he was more Griffin's friend."

"I helped him set up the business side of the café in Southern Pines. Griffin was all about marketing, so Caleb had to deal with all the rest."

"Did you know Caleb is still looking for a place to open a café?"

"He asked if I wanted to partner with him." Suzy scrunched up her face. "He could have at least waited until I buried Griffin."

"This must all be overwhelming. I'll leave you be." I started toward the door, but Suzy pulled me in for a hug.

"I know you're here for information, but it's nice seeing a friendly face. You don't want to kill me." Suzy released me from our embrace and wiped her watery eyes with the back of her hand. "Thanks for coming by."

As I left her shop, I ran through all the motives Suzy mentioned. Of course, she hadn't mentioned her own motives for killing Griffin: jealousy and financial gain. But no matter who was the target, I still didn't know how they got the cyanide into the cup. It was time to see if Rob and Christine had solved that mystery.

27

M y mind was on beignets as I headed toward the police station. Even though it was nearly 2:00 p.m., Christine and Rob would occasionally indulge in an afternoon treat. If I didn't run into them there, I'd take a bag to them. They would see through my "bribe" of the fluffy and sweet beignets, but it didn't hurt to bring them. It would surely soften their annoyance at my questions.

When I was only a block away, my cell phone rang. I expected it to be Connor, checking in from his trip. The name on my phone wasn't his, but Rob's.

"Hi, Rob. Is everything okay?"

"I don't always call you with bad news, do I?"

"No, but last time you called, it was to say Frankie was out of gumbo."

Rob laughed, which I hadn't heard him do since Griffin's death. "No gumbo is bad news. But I'm calling with a serious request."

"I'm all ears." I braced myself for him to tell me not to

talk to the suspects. Had someone called and complained about me?

"Christine and I are asking everyone intimately involved with Griffin's death to meet at the café at five p.m. Since you were near the table and were the first to go to Griffin, we'd like you there."

I breathed a sigh of relief. Well, for a moment I did. "Of course, but can I ask why you want us there?"

"We want to go over that evening, and it will help to have everyone together. You'd be amazed what people remember days later after a crime," Rob said.

"Are you going to share any new information?"

"You'll just have to wait and see. Will you be there?"

Rob's asking was just a formality. He knew I wanted to help Libby. "I'll be there."

This murder resembled an Agatha Christie novel more and more each day. I loved when Poirot would gather the suspects to reveal the killer. But I really shouldn't compare this meeting to a fictional one. Griffin was a human and didn't deserve to die. Hopefully, Rob and Christine would answer all our questions tonight and this tragedy would be finished. Actually, I wanted more than answers—I wanted the murderer arrested.

Going to Café Beignet now was pointless since I had spoken with Rob. Sure, beignets and an iced café au lait would have been delicious, but my stomach was tied up in knots. I had almost three hours to kill before tonight's meetings. Okay, time to kill was not the best phrase to use, but three hours seemed like an eternity.

I used the time to go home and work on the bookshop's

newsletters. With the holidays approaching, I had to sort through the list of new releases and classics to include in our marketing materials. Throwing myself into my work paid off as I knocked off most of my to-do list and forgot about Griffin's death for a few hours. But when my alarm went off at 4:30 p.m., I was more than ready to go to Libby's.

"Sammy, will you let everyone in? I want to keep cleaning the kitchen until Rob and Christine are ready to start?" Libby asked when I arrived at four forty-five.

I came early to see if she needed any help and to make sure she was all right. "I'd be happy to. Anything else I can do?"

"Just keep an eye on everyone. Let Tessa and I know when they're ready to start." Libby joined Tessa in the kitchen.

Winston arrived first. "Are you here with the detectives, or as a suspect?"

"I'm here for Libby, and as far as I know, I'm not a suspect," I said.

"You're not on my list, but I don't know what the police are thinking these days. They're not saying much to the media." Winston took a seat at the table closest to the door.

The next person who arrived also avoided the table where Griffin died. Caleb said a quick hello to me and then joined Winston. They whispered so I couldn't hear their conversation. It abruptly ended with Christine and Rob's arrival. All eyes were on them as they entered the café.

"Thank you all for coming. We're just waiting for Suzy Landry to arrive, correct?" Christine directed her question toward me.

"Yes. I'll go get Libby and Tessa from the kitchen," I said.

I found Libby and Tessa sitting on stools by a prep table.

"Do you remember getting any shipments of the no-calorie sugar in the pink packets?" Libby asked.

"Not at all. We've always had the yellow ones since I started here," Tessa said.

"I'm sorry to interrupt, but Christine and Rob are here." I stepped into the kitchen.

"Sammy, did you just put out any pink sugar packets that night?" Libby stood up and took off her apron.

"No, just yellow ones. But I saw pink ones under the table."

"So that's why the police keep asking about the sweetener packets." Tessa's legs shook slightly as she got up.

"Who brings their own sugar to a coffee shop?" Libby shook her head.

"Someone very picky about their sugar." Tessa hung her apron next to Libby's by the kitchen's exit. "I guess."

I studied Tessa's face as she spoke. The phrase "I guess" seemed like a purposeful afterthought, as if she was covering up her real thoughts: someone she knew brought their own sugar. I couldn't confront her because Christine appeared in the doorway.

"We're all here now, so we need you three to join us."

Tessa left first with Libby. I'd have to wait until after this meeting to talk to Tessa.

Caleb and Winston were now sitting at the table from the night of the murder. Rob escorted Suzy to the table and pulled out the chair for her. The three of them glanced at each other but didn't speak. Christine had Libby go behind the counter, and Tessa and I stood where the table of food had been on that fateful evening.

"Thank you all for being here tonight," Christine said.

"Did we have a choice?" Winston murmured.

Christine gave him one of her steely gazes, and he stared down at the tabletop.

"We hope if we're all together, someone might remember something. Any detail, large or small, is helpful." Rob's voice was soothing, as if he were giving instructions for a party, not a group interrogation.

"Tessa, I have you standing where you were when Griffin collapsed, correct?" Christine asked.

"No, I was behind the counter," Tessa said.

"So you never came out from behind the counter?" Christine said.

"No, I came out to help Sammy with the food and drinks on the big table."

"She did," I said.

"All right, let's have you join Libby behind the counter," Rob said.

Libby put her arm around Tessa when she joined her. They both looked tense as they waited for the detectives to continue.

"Now, for the three of you at the table, did any of you put any of this sugar in your lattes?" Christine sat in Griffin's spot and took two packets of sugar out of the caddy.

All three nodded their heads.

"Did Griffin use the packets, too?" Christine said.

"He only liked the no-calorie sugar." Suzy smiled sadly. "He was a creature of habit. Griffin always put at least three packets in a cup."

"Did anyone see him put the sugar in his mug?" Rob asked.

"No, I didn't," Winston said. "I didn't notice his drink until he said it was the wrong one."

"Same here," Caleb said. "Suzy?"

"I agree. He must have put sugar in it before he said it was almond milk," Suzy said. "He always put more sugar in his than mine. When I took a sip, it was very sweet, and I was pretty sure it was almond milk."

The room was silent, and I believed I wasn't the only one who made the connection. If Griffin insisted on switching the mug after he put sugar in it, could he have been trying to kill Suzy? And if so, what happened?

Winston spoke first. "If I'm putting two and two together, the detectives are saying that Griffin intended to kill Suzy. But he mixed up the sugar packets."

"Or Suzy put poison in her cup, knowing Griffin would switch them if he thought she had the almond milk." Tessa raced over from the counter area, with Libby trailing behind. "You used to bring your own sugar to The Pines Café."

"I only did that when the café was out of fake sugar. I never use the real sugar," Suzy huffed.

Rob put his arm out, so Tessa had to stop before she reached the table. "Now, Tessa, we are just talking right now. We're not accusing anyone of anything."

"Did you analyze the sugar packets and the mugs? How about the coffee that remained on the floor?" I said.

"We are waiting for the results. They should come through before six," Christine said.

"So you got us here to announce the results? What is this, a murder mystery book?" Winston snapped.

"I'd think you'd be happy to be the first to know about the poison." Suzy leaned over the table, her face close to Winston's. "You just love to spread news, whether it's right or wrong."

Winston and Suzy argued with each other while Caleb

tried to interject. Rob and Christine studied them, and I wished I knew who they thought was the killer. Libby had her arm around Tessa, whether to hold her back or comfort her, I wasn't sure. Her face was tense, and I prayed that this would be over soon.

My prayers were answered when Christine's phone rang. With her cell phone pressed against her ear, she hastened to the far corner of the café. She nodded her head as she listened to the caller. Though it seemed like an hour, Christine hung up after just a minute. She waved Rob over, and they huddled together.

Finally, they joined the rest of us. Goose bumps rose on my arms. They must have learned more about the poison or even who the killer was. Nervous anticipation crossed everyone's face.

"We have just learned that there was no cyanide in any of the mugs, packets, or the leftover coffee." Christine slowly paced between Tessa and Libby and the table of suspects. "There was cyanide in Griffin's empty flask. So now I ask all of you, who had drinks with Griffin before the art show?"

28

I wasn't the only one shocked by the news. Everyone started babbling except Rob, Christine, and me. The three of us were spectators. Libby whispered in Tessa's ear and left her to come over to me. She pulled me in for a hug and whispered, "I know it's wrong to feel good about this news, but I can't help it. Thank goodness it wasn't the coffee."

"It's natural to feel that way. I'm relieved for you, too," I whispered back.

"Folks, I realize this is shocking news, but we must ask y'all more questions." Rob's voice rose over the chattering.

"What does this mean?" Suzy asked as the group grew quiet. "They put poison in his flask? So someone wanted to kill Griffin, not me?"

"Did Griffin ever share his flask with anyone?" Rob said.

"No. He drank from it when he thought no one was looking." Suzy's shoulders drooped. "I tried to get him to stop, but he didn't listen. He drank a flask full almost every day."

"So you're saying his flask was poisoned? What about fingerprints on the flask?" Winston sat straight up in his chair. "Since you're not arresting anyone right now, I'll guess there were only Griffin's."

Rob's mouth twitched but he didn't answer Winston.

"Are you going to arrest someone?" Libby asked.

Rob smiled sympathetically at her. "Not right now, Miss Libby. We still have inquiries to make."

Without coming out and saying it, Rob confirmed no one's prints except possibly Griffin's were on the flask. Otherwise, they would have taken that person out for questioning, if not arrested them.

"Knowing who met with Griffin before the show is essential—" Christine started.

"I didn't see him until I got here that night," Suzy interrupted Christine. "I was at work all day. You can check my records and the security camera."

"I didn't see him until the show either." Winston stood up. "Do you want my alibi, too?"

Christine took out her notebook and pointed her pen at Winston. "Since you're offering, yes."

Winston took out his phone and opened a calendar app. "I attended a long and boring city council meeting from nine to noon, and then I had lunch with a friend at Napoleon House. From there, I worked out at my gym and then headed back home to shower. I came to the café after that."

"We'll need the name of your friend," Christine said.

Winston gulped noticeably. "I don't have his number. We just talk when we're at Napoleon House. His name is Greg, I think."

"Uh-huh." Christine scribbled faster in her notebook. "We'll check it out. Now, Caleb, when did you see him?"

"Not until the art show. We had plans to go over our business after the party. I spent the day looking for properties and working in my office. Someone should have seen me around town." Caleb's voice had an undertone of nervousness, which was understandable. Being asked for your alibi for a murder would make anyone nervous except the person with an airtight alibi. He didn't have one, but neither did Winston.

"It's my turn," Libby said. "I didn't meet Griffin until he arrived here at five p.m. Earlier, I worked with two of my bakers here. I left at eleven a.m. for a lunch meeting with a few members of the chamber of commerce until two thirty. My friends walked me back to the café and I stayed here for the rest of the day. I was never alone."

"Thank you, Libby. Can you write their names and numbers for me?" Christine flipped to a new page in her notebook and handed it to Libby.

When she got it back from Libby, Christine continued asking her questions. "Tessa, how about you?"

I held my breath, wondering if Tessa would tell the truth. Would she remember she told me Griffin visited her that day?

"Griffin came to my house around one p.m." Tessa's voice was small.

"What?" Suzy raised her voice. "He saw you, but not me? You two were having an affair, weren't you?"

Christine stepped in front of Suzy. "Miss Landry, I need you to stay calm."

Rob was now by Tessa and continued the questioning. "Tessa, where did you meet Griffin?"

"He came by my house with a painting. It was a gift for helping him get the show here. I had to leave for work, so he only stayed for fifteen minutes," Tessa explained.

"He gave you a painting? I don't believe it," Suzy fumed.

"Well, he did and, like I said, he left. Griffin mentioned

having errands to run before the show. Wasn't seeing his wife one of them?" Tessa's meekness had turned to anger. Her offer to let bygones be bygones with Suzy earlier was undoubtedly canceled.

Suzy shook her head and took a tissue out of her purse. Caleb put his arm around her and she didn't shake it off.

"Does the killer have to be someone who saw him before the show? The cyanide could have been in his flask for days, weeks. If Griffin didn't get to town until the day of the show, his murderer could have done it in Southern Pines. A disgruntled student or a jealous colleague are better suspects than us," Winston said.

"Winston, you were the one who told me Griffin emptied his flask before any major event at the university." Suzy dabbed her eyes and then crumpled the tissue on the table. "I watched him do it. Sometimes he'd refill it twice in one day, especially if he was nervous about a show. The killer must have put the cyanide in the flask that day."

Winston glanced at Tessa, who gave him a sad look. Tessa understood what Winston was doing; he was trying to keep the blame from her. But it didn't work.

"We'll look into all possibilities," Rob said. "No one has been cleared just yet."

"Thank you for coming tonight, and we'll be in touch with everyone tomorrow for your formal statements." Christine snapped her notebook shut.

The group took that as their opportunity to leave. Caleb and Suzy left together, and surprisingly, Tessa agreed to let Winston walk her home. I peered out the window to see all four of them speaking. One day I would learn to lip-read.

"I've never been so happy not to serve alcohol here." Libby joined me at the window.

"Libby, between your alibi and the fact that the crime

scene investigators didn't find any alcohol in the café, I don't think you should worry." Rob walked up to us. "Now, those four are another story."

Although there was no way they could have heard Rob, the group broke up. They left in their original pairs.

"I have to say I'm relieved for me, but it still doesn't make up for the fact Griffin died here. When did he drink from his flask?" Libby said.

"I saw him putting the lid on it when he came out of the bathroom just as the guests were arriving," I said.

"Christine, come here." Rob waved Christine over, who was on her phone again.

She ended her call and came over to us. "What's going on?"

"Sammy, tell her what you told me."

I told Christine about Griffin and his flask. Christine sat down at the nearest table after I finished.

"That matches what the reports say now. They think he would have ingested it no more than thirty minutes before he collapsed," Christine said.

I sat across from her. "Wouldn't he have noticed the taste or the smell? He said he could smell almond milk, so why not the cyanide?"

Christine narrowed her eyes at me. "You do ask good questions: annoying, but good."

"Let me guess. It was something with a potent scent," I said.

"I bet it was amaretto!" Libby pulled a chair up next to me. "I don't make them here, but I've occasionally made amoretti cookies which need amaretto. It's a strong-smelling liquor, for sure."

"You're taking after Sammy, Libby." Christine cracked a

smile for a quick moment. "But yes, traces of amaretto were found in his flask."

"We should follow up on this tomorrow, but let's hit the road for now," Rob said.

"Where are you going?" I asked.

"We're heading to Southern Pines tonight. The president of the university can't meet with us until eight a.m. tomorrow," Rob said. "It was leave before the crack of dawn tomorrow or drive tonight and stay over."

"If either of you remember anything else, don't hesitate to contact us." Christine looked at me. "Don't get into any trouble while we're gone."

"We plan to come back later in the afternoon. Ready to go, Christine?" Rob said.

"Hold it. You'll need food for the drive. Let me get you a box of pastries for the road." Libby jumped up from her chair and went to the counter. "Come pick out what you'd like. It's on the house."

Christine went with Libby, but Rob stayed by me. "Sammy, like Christine said, don't get into any trouble. If you do, I'll make you go to Sissy's next meeting with a wedding planner."

We laughed, but Rob's face didn't hide the seriousness of his and Christine's admonishment not to get into any trouble. I promised everything would be fine while they were gone.

"You better go pick out some cookies, or you'll only have snickerdoodles for the ride," I said.

"Ugh, you're right. Christine, don't you only get snickerdoodles. If you do, I'm playing heavy metal music for the entire ride." Rob went to the bakery counter to negotiate which cookies they were getting.

I accepted a box of scones from Libby, and we all left the

café. After saying goodbye to Rob and Christine, Libby and I walked home.

"I'm sympathetic to all those who cared about Griffin, but I can't deny that I'm relieved my coffee had nothing to do with his death." Libby put her arm through mine as we took our time walking home. The gas lights flickered against the early evening sky as we walked past the shops and art galleries. Musicians packed up their instruments and tip jars while other took their places on the street corner. Tourists searched for restaurants or headed to Bourbon Street for the promise of discount drinks, loud music, joyful dancing, and boisterous crowds.

I preferred the calm environment of Royal Street, which continued as Libby and I entered the courtyard of Thibodeaux Mansion. Libby headed to her apartment with a little more pep in her step. Hopefully tonight she would sleep well, knowing her coffee didn't hold the poison.

But someone put the cyanide in Griffin's flask, and Suzy, Caleb, Winston, and Tessa were still suspects. Hopefully, the list would be narrowed down tomorrow...either by the detectives or me.

29

"Nubi, why did Griffin make a big deal about switching mugs with Suzy? Did he really think he had the wrong drink?"

"Meow." Nubi moved a paw away from his eyes and looked at me. "Meow. Meow."

"You're right. He must have done it for a reason." I scratched Nubi's little white fur patch on his head. He covered his eyes again and settled back into his early evening nap.

I lifted myself from the sofa gradually so as not to bother Nubi again. At least someone was relaxed in this apartment. Finding out the poison wasn't in the mugs should have made me feel better, but it didn't. Libby's exoneration thrilled me. But something still wasn't right about that whole mug exchange Griffin made with Suzy.

And there were the pink packets of sweetener. Tessa claimed Suzy used to bring her own to the café in Southern Pines, but Suzy denied doing it that night. Could Griffin have brought the packets, thinking they were full of cyanide? If so, what happened to the packets? If he had filled them himself, there would have been cyanide in the packets the police tested.

Did he have an accomplice who gave him the sugar packets? Did the killer double-cross Griffin? He looked surprised right before he collapsed, as if he couldn't believe it was happening.

"Nubi, Griffin stared right at the table, so it had to be one of those three, right?" I flopped back on the couch. Nubi didn't move, except his nose twitched. He must be deep into a good dream. I wouldn't dream tonight if I didn't figure out what really happened to Griffin.

I put my tennis shoes back on and grabbed my little blue backpack. A nighttime walk might do me good, especially if I went to see the person I believed was innocent. Hopefully, my intuition was right, otherwise I could be heading to see the killer.

Suzy couldn't be the killer. She had no reason to plan a murder with Griffin. Perhaps if Suzy were involved in Griffin's business, they both would want Caleb dead for the insurance money. But the coffee mug went nowhere near Caleb.

I struggled for a reason for Griffin and Suzy to kill Winston. If Winston had any gossip about either of them, he would have already used it in his blog. And like Caleb, the poisoned mug didn't go near Winston.

And then there was Caleb. The insurance money could have been his motivation. Or again, did he want to cause trouble for Libby so she'd leave the café? If that were the case, he wouldn't have tried to kill Griffin, since they were going to go back into business together.

If my logic was correct, Griffin's partner double-crossed him, and it was either Caleb, Winston, or Tessa. I didn't want to believe Tessa was involved. To kill the man she had a crush on, perhaps loved, was evil. She didn't strike me as the type to plan a murder, but then again, love makes some people do unspeakable things.

It wasn't just her personality that made me doubt she was a killer; the way Griffin looked at the table when he was dying nagged at me. Wouldn't he have stared or called out to Tessa if he thought she'd poisoned him?

Winston's motive could be his love for Tessa, but why would he agree to work with Griffin to kill Suzy in the first place? If he wanted a big sensational story to help his career, killing Suzy or Griffin at a popular café would be it. Again, people do strange things for love or money.

"Hey, Sammy! Whatcha doing on this fine evening?" Brady asked while he tap-danced outside a closed art gallery. He regularly performed at night on Royal Street. During the day, he taught at a dance school.

"Just going for a walk. Looks like you're keeping busy tonight. This mild weather is keeping people out."

"True dat." Brady finished his routine by balancing on the tips of his shoes. "I'll take it over the rain any day. But it feels like rain is coming in tonight. I hope you've got an umbrella in that backpack of yours."

"I don't, so I better get moving before it starts." I dropped a few dollars in Brady's tip bucket. "Don't get those shoes wet. I'll see you later."

"Will do! Thanks, Sammy!" Brady started dancing again as a crowd starting walking toward him.

Chatting with Brady was a lovely reprieve from going over Griffin's murder. As the sound of his tapping faded, I began going over my suspects' motivations.

Caleb had a financial incentive to kill Griffin and Suzy. Murdering Griffin would mean he'd have insurance money for his new business and no partner. Killing Suzy would mean he and Griffin would have more money for their business, too. But the way Caleb was friendly and concerned for Suzy made me doubt he would kill her. Or could he have double-crossed Griffin to get Suzy and the money for himself?

There were so many potential reasons and double crosses with this group, and I needed answers. Suzy seemed to be the right person to talk to now.

When I arrived at Suzy's house, she opened the door before I finished knocking.

"Sammy, you're here, too? I'm popular tonight." Suzy pointed to Tessa, who was taking off her coat. "Come on in."

"Can I come in, too?" Winston, with his gray fedora in his hands, stood behind me.

"Winston, what are you doing here?" Suzy asked.

"I needed to speak to you. We've got to figure out who killed Griffin," he said.

"Funny, that's why Tessa is here, too," Suzy said.

"Tessa, what are you doing here?" Winston asked.

"Like Suzy said, trying to figure out what happened to Griffin." Tessa wrapped her arms around her body.

"Could we come inside? I guess Sammy will want to come in, too." Winston glared at me.

"Yes, let's not do this in front of all my neighbors." Suzy gestured for us to come indoors so Winston and I followed her and Tessa into her living room. This was going to be an interesting gathering, to say the least.

30

Suzy's love of the 1950s extended to her decorating style. The room was filled with mid-century modern furniture, including a tufted turquoise couch and two olive-green side chairs surrounding a low, circular wood coffee table. A record player sat on top of a console table with a stack of records next to it. The yellow walls were empty except for a large atomic clock over the brick fireplace. The last piece of furniture in the room was a glass bar cart.

"You can check the cart for alcohol, but all it has is wine." Suzy pointed at the cart. "I only drink wine, and I didn't keep liquor for Griffin here. It was my way of trying to stop him from drinking when he was here. He wouldn't put wine in his flask."

"I've only seen him put amaretto in his flask. And I never saw him pour any in his coffee." Tessa sat in one of the olive-green chairs.

I kept my face blank, hoping I wouldn't give away that I knew Griffin had amaretto in his flask when he died.

"So, what are you two doing together? I didn't think you

were friendly, especially after tonight's meeting at Libby's," I said.

"I called Suzy to apologize for the way I've been acting toward her. It was immature. I loved Griffin, but he didn't love me back. We never had an affair. I promise." Tessa gripped the sides of the chair but looked directly across at Suzy on the couch.

"I accepted her apology and gave her my own for mistreating her. Griffin was a flirt through and through, but I don't think he had an affair with Tessa or anyone, for that matter." Suzy gulped down a sob. "But I think he tried to kill me with the coffee switch."

Tessa and Winston looked at each other. "Winston, tell Suzy what you told me."

I sat next to Suzy so I could see his face as he spoke. She grabbed my hand and squeezed it tightly.

"I knew Tessa wouldn't have killed Griffin. She's just not that kind of person." He smiled at Tessa. "I'll admit I suspected you first, Suzy. You could have made the switch on purpose, but then Tessa told me Griffin definitely had the almond milk latte."

"How do you know?" I asked.

"I used the cup with the blue line around the rim. The nonfat milks went into the plain white cups. And I checked with Libby, and she swears she gave the mugs to the right people," Tessa said.

"You trust Libby, Sammy, so I'm sure you believe that." Winston raised his eyebrows at me.

"Yes, I trust her implicitly." I nodded. "So Griffin was lying about the almond milk. He had to have changed cups for another reason, like he thought he was putting poison in it. I'm sorry, Suzy."

Suzy released my hand and pulled a tissue from her

skirt pocket. "I've cried about Griffin since I got home, but I'm still in shock. Our marriage wasn't great, but I never thought he'd kill me for money. I was so naïve."

"Griffin always wanted what he wanted no matter who he hurt in the process," Winston said.

"That's exactly what Caleb said tonight. He was devastated that Griffin wanted to kill me." Suzy dabbed her eyes.

"Caleb knew Griffin wanted you dead?" I said. "Why hasn't he told the detectives? Or better yet, why didn't he stop Griffin from trying?"

"Oh, no, he said he knew nothing about Griffin's plan." Suzy widened her eyes. "He just assumed, like all of us, that Griffin tried to kill me."

Tessa and Winston nodded in agreement. Winston reached over and put his hand on Tessa's. She didn't move her hand away, but smiled at him. Did she do that because she was happy for his support, or were they in on Griffin's murder? This wasn't going as well as I had hoped.

"This is all good information, but it still doesn't change the fact Griffin was poisoned from his flask, not a mix-up of the coffee," I said.

"Maybe he put it in the coffee, but did it after he switched them?" Tessa offered. "No, I didn't see him do that, but maybe I missed it."

"Remember the police said there were no traces of the poison in anything but the flask," I said.

The ticking of the clock was the only sound in the room. We sat in total silence. Confusion and fear covered all their faces. With the poison only found in the flask, it was all coming back to who saw Griffin that day. Tessa was the only person who admitted it. And she had a bar cart full of liquor.

But Caleb had his family's heirloom decanter set at his office, too. Did Winston have liquor at his house?

"Sammy, you're staring off into the distance. What's on your mind?" Winston's voice brought me out of my head.

"Was Griffin working alone in this alleged plot to kill Suzy?" I said. "And if not, who would work with him?"

The three of them all protested their innocence simultaneously. I attempted to listen to each of them, but the volume was overwhelming.

"Okay, y'all, you can't talk at once!" I raised my voice. "You three say you're innocent, but you all had reason to kill Griffin. And Caleb did, too. Funny that he isn't here."

"He left just as Tessa arrived, which was only fifteen minutes ago," Suzy said. "He's been such a great friend to me through all this. Griffin and he were best friends."

"He's always liked you, though, Suzy. I remember him always asking for your help at The Pines Café," Tessa said.

"Yes, he needed my help. And no, I don't think he's in love with me, if that's what you're implying." Suzy sat up straight. "He's like a brother to me."

"He asked you to join him in his new business here," I said.

"Well, yes, but that's not a romantic overture," Suzy scoffed.

"Do you have any idea where Caleb was going from here?" Winston asked.

"His house, but let me call him." Suzy took out her cell phone. "Before you say anything, I've had his number for years."

Winston, Tessa, and I stared at Suzy as she called Caleb. "Caleb, it's Suzy. Can you call me when you get this? I'm still at home. Thanks."

"We need to talk to him sooner rather than later," Winston said.

"You really think he would have killed Griffin? But he said he hadn't seen him until the party. Could he have put poison in the flask at the café?" Suzy's voice faltered. "Or do you think he was lying?"

From the look on her face, I think her faith in Caleb was fading, just as it already had for Tessa and Winston.

"Do you know where Caleb lives, Suzy? Why don't I go there now to talk to him?" Winston jumped out of his chair and grabbed his hat from the coffee table.

"You're not going by yourself." Tessa grabbed his hand. "I'm coming with you."

"What if he's the killer? I don't want you getting hurt." Winston put his hat on with his free hand.

"I don't want you getting hurt either. We'll just go talk to him." Tessa let go of his hand and stood up. She covered her mouth as she coughed. "Let's go."

"Tessa, that cough sounds pretty bad," Winston said.

"I'm fine..." Tessa coughed again, and her face turned red. She sat back down. "Let me just catch my breath."

"No, you're not." Winston crouched in front of her. "You need to relax, or your asthma will get worse. I'll go get Caleb to come back here and we'll all talk. How's that?"

"Let me get you some water, Tessa." Suzy left the room.

"Sammy, you'll keep an eye on Tessa for me." Winston's voice made it clear this was a demand, not a question.

"I'm not a child, Winston." Tessa frowned.

"Sorry, I didn't mean to offend you. I'm just worried about you," Winston said.

Tessa nodded and inhaled deeply. "I'm fine, really."

"I'll keep calling him, but here's Caleb's address." Suzy left the room and came back with a piece of paper and a bottle of water. "If you get ahold of him before me, tell him to come here. All of us can talk this through."

"Sure." Winston took the address from Suzy. "I'll call you as soon as I find him."

Suzy headed over to her bar cart and poured herself a glass of red wine. She returned to the sofa and sipped it.

"I'll be right back, Suzy." I followed Winston outside and stopped him before he left.

"Listen, are you sure about finding Caleb? Rob and Christine will talk to him tomorrow," I said.

"But what if he leaves town? I need to find him tonight," Winston said.

"Are you sure this isn't for an exclusive article? You're not even sure he killed Griffin," I said.

"Are you trying to stop me from going because you want to be the one to solve the murder?" A vein in Winston's neck throbbed.

"Actually, I don't want to see you get into trouble if Caleb is the murderer." I put my hands on my hips.

"That'll be a first. You actually being nice to me," Winston grunted. "Or are you worried I'm the killer?"

Before I could speak, Winston stomped away. He was right, though. I was concerned he could be the killer. If he intended to murder Caleb, three witnesses knew he planned to meet him. Hopefully, if he found Caleb, he'd let him know we knew where he was. Or could they both be in on it?

A headache hit me like a brick. Maybe I should have asked for a glass of wine from Suzy.

I went back inside to find Tessa and Suzy sitting together on the couch. Suzy had her arm around Tessa, who was wheezing.

"Tessa, you don't sound good at all. Do you need a doctor? I can call my friend Sissy, who is a nurse," I said.

"No, I'll be fine. I guess I'm more stressed about this whole situation than I realized." Tessa took a sip from the water bottle Suzy had given her. "And now I'm worried about Winston."

"He is stubborn, to say the least, but I'm sure he'll take care of himself," Suzy said sympathetically.

"Sammy, I didn't kill Griffin and I know Winston didn't. I don't believe Suzy did it, either, so that just leaves Caleb." Tessa coughed again. "Winston wants to get the story first, but we all want to clear our names."

"I can't believe Caleb would do this, but I agree we all need to talk," Suzy said.

Tessa began wheezing again. "Can you hand me my purse, Sammy?"

I grabbed Tessa's purse from the floor and gave it to her. She rustled around in it, her movements becoming more frantic as she did. "My inhaler isn't in here."

"Check your pockets," Suzy said.

Tessa did but came up empty. "It must be at home. I switched purses, and I must have left it in the other one. I need to go."

"I'll go with you," I said.

"Thanks, but I can do it." Tessa went to stand up, but a coughing fit made her sit back down.

"Is your roommate home? Could she bring it here?" I said.

"No, she's at work. I'll just go." Tessa's coughing fit returned.

"Let me get it for you. I can run there and be back quickly." I put my backpack on and put out my hand. "I just need your key."

"Thanks." Tessa croaked and handed me her key. She leaned back against the sofa with her eyes closed.

Suzy followed me to the front door. "Come back soon."

"I will, but if her wheezing gets worse, call nine-one-one," I said.

"Yes, I'll do that if needed." Suzy leaned in close. "But hurry back because I'm worried about Winston finding Caleb. What if Winston is the killer, and he tries to frame Caleb?"

Suzy's faith in Caleb clearly had returned. For her sake, I hoped Caleb wasn't the killer. Then again, for Tessa's sake, I hoped Winston wasn't the killer either. I couldn't stay and placate Suzy's concerns. Tessa's cough hadn't stopped, so I needed to go.

"We'll all talk about this when I get back. Just keep Tessa calm and call an ambulance if you're worried. Better safe than sorry."

Suzy nodded and closed the door behind me. I ran toward Tessa's house, thankful that my running pace had improved since moving to New Orleans. Getting Tessa's inhaler to her was my first priority, but after that, I needed to solve this mystery once and for all.

31

Very few cars or pedestrians were out as I ran to Tessa's home. I sprinted across the streets and down the sidewalks, but I had to keep my eye out for any uneven pavement and sidewalks. I reached Tessa's house quickly, but I was breathless. I huffed and puffed as I unlocked the front door. The porch light wasn't on, so I had a hard time seeing the lock. Finally, the key went in and I opened the door.

"Hello? Lori, are you home?" I locked the door behind me and stepped into the living room. Tessa mentioned that Lori was at work, but I called out just to be sure in case she was here. I didn't need her thinking I was a thief, or worse, a killer, coming after Tessa or her. No one responded, and the only sounds in the house was the hum of the refrigerator in the kitchen.

I forgot to ask Tessa where she had left her purse, so I might have to search the entire home. That wasn't necessary, as her purse lay on the coffee table in the living room. I needed to get back to Tessa, but I had one more thing to do here. I put my backpack by Tessa's purse and went to check the bar for amaretto.

A smart killer wouldn't keep the liquor they used to poison someone, especially if the cyanide was in the actual bottle. Tessa may have added cyanide to Griffin's flask before the liquor. I didn't have time to search the house for cyanide, but I could look at the bar.

I wanted to check out Caleb and Winston's houses, too. Caleb's office also needed to be checked. I promised Rob and Christine I wouldn't get in trouble, so I wouldn't break into their places.

It'd be easy to check Caleb's office. I could lie again about looking for real estate and get him to offer me a drink. But I wouldn't drink it, especially if it was the type of liquor that killed Griffin. But seeing Winston's home would be harder. I might have to let the detectives handle that. But then again, they were out of town tonight.

But for now, I focused on Tessa's bar. All the bottles had their original labels, so I quickly scanned them. There was whiskey, bourbon, absinthe, gin, tequila, rum, brandy, and three kinds of vodka. There was no amaretto, and nothing looked missing since my last visit. Not that this proved anything definitively, but I felt a little better about Tessa.

Just as I went to grab my backpack and Tessa's purse, the front doorknob rattled. Was Lori coming home? Goose bumps rose on my arms as I heard a man grunt as the front door flew open. I didn't have time to react before Caleb stumbled into the house with his lockpick set in one hand and a large shopping bag in the other.

32

———

"Oh, Sammy, why did you have to be here?" Caleb closed the door behind him and locked it. He placed the duffel bag on the floor and shoved the lockpick set in his pocket. "Tessa is at Suzy's, and her roommate is working, so I expected the house to be empty. This complicates my plans."

I balled my hands into fists and pressed them into the sides of my legs, hoping Caleb wouldn't see my hands shaking. Caleb's usual pleasant smile was gone and replaced by an angry, tight-lipped frown. His tall and solid frame caught my attention as he blocked the front door. Pushing him aside and running away wouldn't work. Could I make it to the back door without him catching me? I doubted it, but that might be my only option.

Caleb took that choice away from me when he pulled a gun out of his jacket pocket.

"I just planned to leave the poisoned liquor, but now I have to deal with you." Caleb shook his head, but the hand holding the gun was steady. "Let's go into the living room. I assume that's where Tessa's bar is."

That also was where my purse with my cell phone and pepper spray was. Not that either would be a match for his weapon. For now, I had no choice but to go along with Caleb's demands.

"Let me guess. The duffel bag has the decanter with amaretto and cyanide in it." I went over to the bar cart. "Tessa and Lori own all kinds of alcohol except amaretto. There's not even room for you to put a bottle here."

Caleb kept the gun on me as he carried his bag over to me. He unzipped it and took out his decanter bottle with a shaky hand. "I was going to pour out the poisoned liquor into her bottle. I can't believe she doesn't own it. As much as she loved Griffin, I assumed she had it here for him."

"Like Suzy, I imagine she didn't keep it so Griffin wouldn't drink more of it. Unlike you, they cared about Griffin's health."

"Well, they didn't have to deal with Griffin like I did." Caleb held the decanter tightly against his chest. The gun trembled slightly in his hands. "Being his business partner was living hell. He had no concept of money and just wanted everything his way."

"So that's why you killed him instead of Suzy?"

Caleb's eyes widened. "You figured that out?"

"Griffin's performance gave it away. He made a big deal about switching the coffee mugs. My guess is the poison was supposed to be in his cup and he would give it to Suzy. But you double-crossed him, didn't you?" I hoped my voice sounded stronger than my body felt. I refused to give up on finding an escape, even in the face of the pointed gun. Keeping him talking was my only solution right now.

Caleb put the decanter on the floor. "Yes, that was *his* plan. He bought another insurance policy on Suzy so there would be enough money to buy a gallery and café here."

"Why would you kill Suzy for money? You seem to care about her."

"I do, but Griffin had me between a rock and a hard place. I'm broke. You saw my pathetic office. It was the only place that would rent to me. I'm up against experienced agents here, so it'll take years to build up my real estate business."

"So you agreed to help Griffin kill his wife for money? You could have said no. You should have turned him in to the police."

"I had no evidence. It would just be my word against his."

"But you changed the plan. You poisoned Griffin instead of Suzy. Did you give him real sugar packets instead of ones filled with cyanide?" I took a step away from the cart, planning to work my way nonchalantly toward the couch.

"Yes, the plan was I'd give him the poison in sugar packets. Griffin was mad when he saw I used the wrong color packets. Is that how you figured out that's where the poison would be?" Caleb tilted his head to the side.

I nodded. "I assumed you slipped him the packets either earlier or at the table. Just before Griffin collapsed, he stared back at the table, and that's when he realized you had betrayed him."

"I was so worried he would call out my name, but he didn't get a chance. I gave him enough cyanide to kill him quickly."

"Where did you get the cyanide? From the photography supplies the former tenant left in your office?"

Caleb's eyes widened. "You figured that out, too? People told me you were clever, but I can't believe you thought of that."

"If I came up with that theory, so will the detectives."

This wasn't the time to toot my own horn about being correct about the source of the poison.

"My landlord is taking the boxes away tomorrow, so there will be no proof I had access to cyanide." Caleb regained a bit of his confidence and puffed out his chest.

"You're taking an enormous risk that your landlord won't say anything about the supplies when the detectives come around." I didn't tell Caleb I would tell the police, too. He might just shoot me now if I reminded him I had solved the mystery. I needed to keep him talking until I came up with a way to escape. I struggled to hold in my fears, but it was getting harder and harder not to cry or keep my body from shaking.

"Everything about this whole plan has been a huge risk. Griffin loved taking risks. He blamed me when our café went belly-up, but he was just as responsible for it as me."

Caleb shuffled from side to side as his face turned a shade of purple I hadn't even seen during Mardi Gras. I had to get him calm again so he would keep confessing.

"You knew he'd empty his flask before the show. Griffin was a creature of habit when it came to drinking amaretto," I said.

"I hope he realized what I had done before he died. He deserved it for all the pain he caused," Caleb snarled. "He treated Suzy like dirt, and he strung Tessa along for years."

"Why are you here trying to frame Tessa, then?" I snapped.

"I have no other choice. She admitted she saw Griffin that afternoon. Winston has an alibi, and I'd never hurt Suzy." The desperation in Caleb's voice would have made me sympathetic if he wasn't a murderer.

"Griffin must have come to you that afternoon. You refilled his flask for him."

"Yes, I said we needed to seal the plan to kill Suzy and I always drink to close a deal. It almost didn't work." Caleb shook his head. "He said he couldn't since he had to meet Tessa. I offered to fill his flask. Of course he said yes. Free liquor was his favorite."

"Since your prints weren't on the flask, how did you manage that? You would have handed it to him." I squeezed my eyes together as I imagined the scene at Caleb's office. Then it hit me. "Let me guess, you wiped off the flask when your back was to him. You put the flask on a stack of folders and put them on your desk. Griffin then picked it up."

"I can't believe you got that right." Caleb's voice quivered. "Yes, that's what I did. Griffin thought nothing about it. He snatched his flask and left to go see Tessa to give her a painting. I actually believe he cared for her and gave her the painting as a kind gesture."

"But Tessa would be—she was—a prime suspect! That's not kindness," I scoffed.

"No, it wasn't, but Griffin only cared about himself. He hoped Tessa wouldn't be implicated, but he couldn't resist the opportunity to kill Suzy in a public place where it looked like he was the intended victim."

I took another step toward the couch as Caleb closed his eyes. Despite my body's urge to run, I knew Caleb would shoot if I did. My only hope was to keep him talking, and he seemed to want to confess to me.

"You realize someone must have seen you and Griffin together. Rob and Christine are incredible detectives, and they'll keep on the case until they get the evidence."

Caleb opened his eyes and glared at me. "That's why I have to frame Tessa. I can just say I was too scared to admit I saw Griffin. But if Tessa has the poisoned amaretto, the police will have to arrest her."

"But she doesn't have a bottle of amaretto. You'll have to leave the decanter here. Are you really going to give up a piece of your great-grandfather's set?"

For the first time since he arrived, Caleb let down his defenses. His shoulders sank and his eyes watered. But he didn't put down the gun. "I'll just find something in her kitchen to put it in. I've got to improvise."

"You're taking an enormous risk here. What if Tessa or her roommate finds it first?"

"I need you to be quiet." Caleb's frustration resonated in his voice. "Sammy, stop moving. Don't think I haven't noticed you stepping toward the couch."

I remained silent as Caleb tapped his foot and he furrowed his brow. This was my chance to look around the room for a weapon. I could throw a liquor bottle at him, but I wasn't sure that would be enough of a distraction for me to get away.

Caleb finally spoke, "You are a good detective, Sammy. I didn't know how you'd solved other mysteries in town until after Griffin was dead. But I had to do it even if someone like you was there."

The wailing of a police car or fire truck startled me, and I jumped. Griffin went to one of the front windows and pulled back the curtain. With the sirens fading, Griffin turned his attention back to me. "Why are you here? Did you break in to find the poison?"

My stomach flip-flopped as my hope for help coming here faded. I just had to keep him talking. I hoped Tessa was okay without her inhaler. But maybe she or Suzy would send Winston to come check on me. For once, I wanted Winston here, or anyone, for that matter.

"Tessa needs her inhaler, and I came to get it. She gave

me her key." I took the key out of my pocket. "They know I'm here."

"I wish you had broken in here on your own." Caleb shook his head. "I need to rethink this."

Caleb gripped the gun tightly in his hand as he paced. As organized as he had been to kill Griffin, now he looked like he was grasping at straws. The more he marched back and forth, the more he loosened his grip on the gun. I took a chance that I could cause a distraction and he would drop the gun.

"Caleb, Tessa's roommate will be here soon. You can leave before she gets here," I said.

"But there's still the problem of what to do with you, Sammy. I don't want to kill you..." Caleb shook his head.

"Do you hear that? I can hear footsteps outside the door. Lori must be home," I lied.

"What? No, it's too early!" Caleb turned to face the door, and I took advantage of it.

I pushed him with all my might, and Caleb crashed to the floor. The gun fell out of his hand, but skittered across the floor ten feet away. I wouldn't be able to get it without stepping over him, and I'm sure he would have grabbed me. I made a split-second decision and picked up Caleb's decanter from the floor.

"Sammy, you liar!"

Before Caleb could turn over, I smashed the decanter over his head. Caleb remained motionless as the glass shattered around him. He was still breathing, so I hadn't killed him, thank goodness. I just needed him unconscious long enough for me to call the police. Kicking the gun down the hall, I took out my phone and dialed 9-1-1.

"This is how *I* seal a deal, Caleb."

33

The first police car arrived in just a few minutes. An ambulance soon followed.

"Miss Richardson, what in the world happened here?" Officer Adams stooped by Caleb's body as he stirred. "Are you okay? I'm assuming you hit him over the head with that bottle."

Caleb's crystal decanter lay scattered across the floor. The poisoned liquor dripped down his head and onto the floor.

"I did it to protect myself. His gun is over there." I pointed to the revolver down the hall. "Be careful around the liquid. It's poisoned with cyanide."

"Thanks for the heads-up." Officer Adams stood up and waved the paramedics in. "Be careful y'all with that liquid. It's supposedly poisoned."

"You can wipe it off his face, but we'll need the crime scene investigators to take samples of the liquor." Christine walked into the house. "Sammy, I'm glad you're standing, unlike Caleb."

Caleb woke up as the paramedics started checking him.

They flipped him over, and his eyes fluttered and then focused on the ceiling.

"Sir, can you hear me? I'm wiping the liquid off your face. Do not swallow." The paramedic took a gauze pad from his kit and wiped Caleb's face.

"Ugh, m-my head is killing me," Caleb stuttered as his face was cleaned. "Griffin ruined my life."

I breathed a sigh of relief that Caleb was conscious and speaking. I admit I was a little surprised he said Griffin ruined his life and not me. Not that I cared if Caleb blamed me for getting caught.

"Christine, I thought you and Rob were on your way to Southern Pines," I said.

"We hadn't left yet when Suzy called us. She was worried you hadn't returned with Tessa's inhaler," Christine said.

Rob put his arm around me, and I leaned against him. "Luckily, we were still at the station gathering our things when we received the call. Suzy was frantic about you."

"You've saved us a trip to Southern Pines." Christine took gloves and picked up Caleb's gun and emptied the bullets. "You're lucky Caleb didn't use this loaded gun, Sammy."

I shuddered as my adrenaline faded. The reality that Caleb brought a loaded gun to Tessa's house meant he had been willing to kill Tessa and her roommate if necessary. Caleb moaned as the paramedics loaded him on the gurney.

"I'll go with him to the hospital." Christine handed the evidence bags with the unloaded gun and bullets to Rob. "Sammy, I'll be interested to hear what transpired here. Rob, I'll meet with you later."

Christine squeezed my shoulder before she left with the

paramedics and Caleb. Rob guided me into the living room as the crime scene investigators filled the house.

"Rob, is Tessa okay?" My heart skipped a beat, realizing I'd left Tessa without her inhaler.

"Yes, Suzy remembered she had a neighbor who had asthma, and he brought over a new inhaler." Rob sat next to me on the sofa. "Tessa is on her way to the hospital to be evaluated. Suzy went with her."

"That's a relief. Tessa and Suzy might become friends after this. It'll be interesting to see what happens with Winston and Tessa."

"I don't know if they'll get back together. However, Winston went to the hospital to meet Tessa and Suzy instead of coming here. That says something. There might be at least one happy ending to this tragedy." Rob stood up and kissed the top of my head. "Besides the fact you're alive."

"Thanks, Rob."

"Wait here, and I'll drop you at home after I get your complete statement. But in the meantime, you better answer all your texts. Suzy also called Libby and the Thibodeaux Mansion group text is blowing up."

I grabbed my backpack and reached in for my cell phone. Sure enough, there were already thirty messages in the text chain and ten missed calls. I messaged the group: *I'm OK. The killer has been caught and Rob will bring me home soon. Don't worry about me.*

I leaned back on the couch as the organized chaos of the investigation surrounded me. Tears welled up in my eyes as relief washed over me. This murder was solved without any other bloodshed. Well, except Caleb's head, but that didn't count. The other suspects had been proven innocent, and that's all that mattered to me.

34

Two days after Caleb and my confrontation, Libby had a small gathering at the café after it closed. She hesitated to call it a party, but wanted a gathering to put the murder behind everyone involved.

Winston and Tessa held hands as they entered the café. Suzy followed behind with a smile on her face.

"I'm happy Winston and Tessa found each other again." Suzy joined me at a table as Tessa and Winston walked directly to Libby.

"They do seem happy together," I said.

"You should have seen how worried Winston was at the hospital that night. When Tessa asked him to stay with her while waiting for the doctor, he lit up like a Christmas tree." Suzy took a tissue from her purse and dabbed her eyes. "I hope they'll do better than Griffin and I did."

After Caleb recovered from his concussion, he confessed to the murder scheme Griffin had planned. He admitted to double-crossing Griffin and his subsequent plan to frame Tessa. He denied he would have used the gun against Tessa or me, but he had no excuse for why he brought it with him that night.

Suzy reacted as I expected. She cried, wailed, and raged about Griffin when Rob and Christine explained what had happened. Suzy did the same about Caleb, although she had a bit of sympathy for him.

"If Caleb had just come to me, we could have stopped all of this. Griffin and I would have divorced, but he would be alive," Suzy had said to the detectives. "And Caleb wouldn't be spending the rest of his life in prison."

Tonight Suzy appeared more sad than angry about Griffin and Caleb. "I don't know how I'm going to get over this."

I put my hand over Suzy's. "You'll keep going with your plans for your life. They won't have Griffin in them, but you'll find love again. If you want to, that is. For now, just concentrate on you and the people who care about you."

"Thank you, Sammy. I'm glad to have you and Andrew in my life." Suzy smiled.

"You have all of us, Suzy!" Libby took the seat in between Suzy and me. "We're all family here in the French Quarter. Don't think you're alone."

I left Libby and Suzy to talk. If anyone could reassure her, it was Libby. Winston and Tessa were picking out cookies as I walked past them. Their heads were close together as they looked over the table. I didn't want to interrupt them, so I headed toward Connor, who was in front of Terry's painting of him and me.

Winston stopped me when I was halfway there. "Hey, Sammy. Can we talk for a minute?"

"Sure." I braced myself for a snarky remark about my confrontation with Caleb and how it could have gone wrong. Instead, Winston wrapped his arms around me. He pulled away after a few seconds and smiled. "I wanted to thank you for clearing Tessa's name."

"Oh, you're welcome." I stared at him, not sure if I was more surprised about his hug or his admission of gratitude. But he returned to his normal self.

"You beat me this time, but that's okay." He smiled.

"Really? That doesn't sound like you. Are you feeling all right?"

"I have Tessa back in my life, and that's worth more than finding the killer before you."

"Wow. Winston has a heart." I grinned. "Really, I'm happy for you both."

Winston took off his hat and bowed. He walked back to Tessa and put his arm around her. Tessa deserved happiness after all of this, and I hoped Winston would give her what she needed. After she came home from the hospital, she called me to thank me for all I had done. I apologized for the mess I made, but she didn't mind. She hoped the amaretto smell wouldn't linger in the house for too long.

I joined Connor at our painting and put my arm around his waist. "Why does the painting say sold? Terry claimed it would be a gift when we got engaged."

"I asked him about it. He said Momma had to put a sold sign on it so people would stop asking to buy it. It's still a gift when we get engaged." Connor put his arm around my shoulder and pulled me tight against him. "No rush for us to become betrothed."

"Sounds good to me. We've got to get Rob and Sissy married first, before anyone else." I laughed.

"If Rob keeps getting all these cases, it might be awhile. And Sissy, too, since she's become one of your partners in crime."

"And are you the other partner?"

"Maybe." Connor winked. "All I know is the next mystery to solve is what to get you for your birthday. It's not too far away."

"Your mom has offered to throw a party here, but I said no. She's busy enough with the reopening."

Connor laughed. "Is that the real reason? Or are you trying to get out of having a party?"

"Oh, no, I love birthday parties." I got on my tiptoes to kiss Connor. "I just don't want to tempt fate with another corpse in the café."

Sammy's New Orleans adventures continue in
Happy Homicide

Don't forget to check out Libby's Scone Recipe!

LIBBY'S SWEET POTATO SCONES
RECIPE

Libby's Sweet Potato Scones
makes 8

Scones
2 cups all-purpose flour
2 1/2 tsp baking powder
1 tsp ground cinnamon
2 tsp pumpkin pie spice
1/2 tsp salt
1/2 cup browned butter made from 3/4 cup butter, chilled
1/3 cup + 2T heavy whipping cream
1 large egg
1/2 cup sweet potato puree
1/2 cup brown sugar
1 tsp pure vanilla extract
1 cup pecans, toasted and chopped *(optional)*
Course sugar *(optional)*

Drizzle *(optional)*
1 cup powdered sugar

1/4 cup sweet potato purée
1 tsp cinnamon
pinch of salt

Instructions

1. The morning of or even the day before, melt the 3/4 cup butter in a heavy bottomed sauce pan over medium heat. Gently stir the butter as it melts and begins to brown; do not take your eyes off of the pan. Continue to stir until the butter reaches a deep, golden brown. Pour into a heat safe container, cool, and put in the refrigerator or freezer to completely chill.
2. Adjust your oven backing rack to the middle position and preheat the oven to 400°F/204°C.
3. Line a baking sheet with parchment paper or silicone mat and set aside.
4. In a large bowl, whisk together the flour, baking powder, cinnamon, pumpkin pie spice, and salt.
5. Roughly chop the chilled butter and add to the dry ingredients.
6. Using a pastry cutter or fork, cut in the cold butter until it's pea sized and crumbly. You can use your fingers but work quickly so the butter doesn't become warm. If it does, pop the bowl into the refrigerator for 10 minutes to chill again and then continue.
7. In a separate bowl, whisk together the 1/3 cup heavy whipping cream, egg, sweet potato puree, brown sugar, and vanilla extract.
8. Pour the cream mixture over the dry ingredients and stir until just combined.
9. Add the chopped nuts and stir again.
10. Transfer the dough to a lightly floured surface and gently knead to bring it together into a ball.

11. Pat the dough into an 8 inch circle and then cut it into 8 equal wedges with a sharp knife.
12. Place the scones two inches apart on the prepared baking sheet.
13. Brush the top of each scone with the remaining heavy cream and lightly sprinkle with course sugar.
14. Bake for 20-25 minutes or until the scones are lightly browned.
15. While the scones cool on a rack, prepare the drizzle.
16. Combine all the drizzle ingredients in a bowl and mix until smooth. You may have to add more sugar or puree to get it to the consistency of honey.
17. When the scones are completely cool, use a spoon to drizzle each scone.

These scones can be stored in an airtight container for up to 2 days but they are best enjoyed right away with a cafe au lait!

Recipe by Leann Mullender of Sammsterdam; adapted from Sally's Baking Addiction

ACKNOWLEDGMENTS

As always, thank you to my husband and children for all their love, support, and ideas for my books.

Thank you to Dipper and Mabel, the sweetest cats, who inspire my fictional cats.

Dad and Wanda, you're always there to support me and lend an ear. It means the world.

My critique group continues to listen to my wild ideas and help shape them into an actual novel. I'm thankful we're still together after five years!

A huge thank you to the most amazing beta-readers, Chrystal, Leann, and Jenna. An extra shout-out to Chrystal, who not only reads my books, but listens to my ramblings and supports me as a fellow writer.

Libby's sweet potato scones would not exist without the incredible talents of Leann of Sammsterdam! Thanks for helping me with the recipe and teaching me how to bake. Sammy and I both have a long way to go!

Thank you to my family, friends, and readers for being here for me and my books!

ABOUT THE AUTHOR

Jen Pitts is a lifelong mystery reader who turned her obsession into writing cozy mysteries of her own. When she isn't plotting fictional murder, she's chugging coffee, traveling to New Orleans, reading, and enjoying life with her husband, children, and two cats in the Pacific Northwest.

Learn more about Jen through her newsletter. A free short story prequel is available exclusively for newsletter members. Sign up at www.jenpittsauthor.com

And keep up daily with Jen on Facebook where she shares her books, her cats, and her love of New Orleans.

You can also find Jen on the following social media sites:

facebook.com/jenpittsmysteryauthor

instagram.com/jenpittsmysterywriter

goodreads.com/jenpitts

amazon.com/author/jenpitts

bookbub.com/authors/jen-pitts

ALSO BY JEN PITTS

The French Quarter Mystery Series:

Coffee, a Scone, and a Place to Call Home - a Short Story Prequel

The Key to Murder

The Gates to the Afterlife

A Deadly Check-In

Bury the Past

The Dead End Tour

A Corpse in the Cafe

Happy Homicide

The Witches of the French Quarter Series:

Mardi Gras and Magic

Red Beans and Rituals